## An Invitation to Trouble!

Trisha Royce came up to Sam in the Palm Pavilion's lobby. "Are you off work?" she asked Sam. Sam nodded. "Want to come to my house for a dip in the pool?"

Sam hesitated. She didn't want to hurt Liza and Chris by leaving with Trisha two days in a row. Still, she was eager to see the elegant Royce house.

Liza took the problem out of her hands. "We'd love to come," she said. "Wouldn't we, Chris?"

"Absolutely," Chris agreed. "We'd love to."

Sam felt her stomach tighten, but she wasn't sure why. Why should it make her tense to spend the afternoon with two old friends and a new one? She didn't know the answer, but something inside told her that this afternoon was going to be bad news.

**Look for these other books in the
SITTING PRETTY series:**

# *SITTING PRETTY*
# TRUE BLUE

by Suzanne Weyn

**Troll Associates**

# For Diana

*Library of Congress Cataloging-in-Publication Data*

Weyn, Suzanne.
 True blue / by Suzanne Weyn; illustrated by Joel Iskowitz.
  p.  cm.—(Sitting pretty; #2)
  Summary: Sam jeopardizes her babysitting job at the Palm Pavilion
Hotel and her friendship with Chris and Liza when she befriends
sophisticated Trisha Royce who believes in winning at all costs.
  ISBN 0-8167-2005-3 (lib. bdg.)  ISBN 0-8167-2006-1 (pbk.)
  [1. Friendship—Fiction. 2. Hotels, motels, etc.—Fiction.
3. Babysitters—Fiction.] I. Iskowitz, Joel, ill. II. Title.
III. Series: Weyn, Suzanne. Sitting pretty; #2.
PZ7.W539Tr 1991
[Fic]—dc20         90-10830

A TROLL BOOK, published by Troll Associates,
Mahwah, NJ 07430

# Chapter One

"I can't believe you let this chain get so rusty," said Samantha O'Neill as she knelt and oiled the chain of her friend Chris's old three-speed bicycle. The chain had jammed as Sam, Chris Brown and their friend, Liza Velez, were riding up the dirt road which led to the Palm Pavilion Hotel.

"*I* can't believe you carry a can of oil with you," said Chris, standing beside her. "You're not a Girl Scout anymore. You don't always have to be prepared!"

"Sam and I were both in the same Brownie troop," Liza said. She knelt beside her bike and tied the yellow laces of her pink high-top sneakers. "Then the troop leader moved and no one ever replaced her. Do you remember Mrs. Gordon, Sam? She always wore that funny plaid shorts set with the matching hat."

Sam looked up from the chain and smiled. "Mrs.

1

Gordon was nice, though. I liked Girl Scouts. I don't see anything wrong with being prepared. If I didn't have this oil in my basket, what would you do now, Chris?"

"Cry," Chris admitted. "Mr. Parker already thinks I'm a flake. If I was late, I think he'd fire me on the spot."

Sam smoothed back her long ash-blond ponytail and glanced down at her plastic watch. "Shoot! We're all going to be fired if we don't get moving. It's eight-twenty!" She slid the chain forward on its track. "I think it's okay now. Try it," she told Chris.

Chris hopped onto her bike and pedaled forward. "Perfect," she announced. "Thanks."

"Ready for another exciting day at the Palm Pavilion Hotel?" asked Liza, tucking a few stray strands of her long brown hair back into her headband before speeding off.

The three girls raced toward the large, rose-colored hotel. They were spending their summer there working as baby sitters for the children of many of the wealthy customers. Mr. Parker, the hotel's manager, kept a sharp eye on them, since they were the youngest and newest of the hotel's more than two hundred employees.

Though it was early, the hot Florida sun was already starting to burn away the dewy coolness of the morning. Sam narrowed her green eyes and squinted into the sun. Every time she saw the hotel, she felt as if she was approaching a fairy tale king-

2

dom. Every window in the massive building sparkled in the sunlight. The flaps of its crisp white awnings fluttered gently, blown by the whispering breezes from the crystal blue ocean just behind it.

They'd had the job for only two weeks, but so far Sam thought that working at the exclusive Palm Pavilion was the greatest thing that had ever happened in all her fourteen years. She loved everything about it: taking care of the kids; seeing the sometimes famous, always rich, customers; feeling that she was somehow part of this cool, luxurious haven that was a direct contrast to her slightly run-down, quiet home town of Bonita Beach.

They turned into the entrance and walked their bikes up past the tall palm trees that lined the long, white-gravel drive that led to the hotel. Only the grounds keepers were out and about, riding their power mowers, cutting the lush green grass of the huge golf course which lay off to the right.

"Fore!" a man shouted. The girls heard the sharp thwack of a golf club hitting the ball off a tee. Sam turned and saw a man in a white shirt and canary yellow pants shield his eyes and try to see where his ball had landed.

"The only guests who get up before nine in this hotel are the golf fanatics," Chris commented. "They probably get up at dawn or something."

"That's because it gets too hot out there if they start any later," Sam reasoned.

3

"Golf seems like the most boring game in the world," said Liza. "What's so much fun about it?" she asked, turning to Sam.

Sam shrugged. "I don't know. I never played golf."

Liza pretended to stumble back into her bike. She held her hand to her forehead dramatically, her large brown eyes wide with mock horror. "There is actually a sport on this earth that you — Miss Athlete of All Time — haven't tried!" she cried. "I don't believe it! I'm in shock. I think I'm going to faint."

"Cut it out!" Sam said, smiling. "There are lots of sports I've never tried."

"Name one," Chris challenged.

"Hang-gliding, parachute-jumping, surfing — "

"You surfed last summer," Chris interrupted.

"I only got up on my knees, then Lloyd wanted his board back."

Chris's hazel eyes suddenly lit up mischievously. "Speaking of Lloyd, I've been meaning to ask you a favor. Do you think you could ask Lloyd — "

"No," said Sam, shaking her head.

"You don't even know what I'm going to ask!" Chris protested. The girls parked their bikes in the rack at the side of the hotel.

Sam took a chain and lock from her basket and looped it through the wheels, chaining all three bikes together. "I don't want to ask Lloyd any-thing," she said. "It's bad enough that guy is at my

4

house every day with his head stuck in the refrigerator. I don't have to talk to him, too."

"He's awfully cute," said Liza, heading over to the service entrance of the hotel. "Your sister Greta has excellent taste in boyfriends."

"Excellent taste?" cried Sam. "That guy has the brain of a flea. All he thinks about is surfing, surfing, surfing."

"Speaking of surfing!" Chris continued as she and Sam followed Liza up the walkway. "I know that he surfs every day over at Castaway Cove. All I want you to ask him is if he would come over and talk to us if we went down there tomorrow. No big deal."

Sam's brow furrowed in a skeptical expression. "Why do I get the feeling that this has something to do with Bruce Johnson?"

"Because you're a genius," said Chris. "*And* one of my very best friends in the whole world. Come on, Sam, I know you'd be thrilled to help me with something so important."

"What do you have in mind?" Sam laughed as she yanked open the screen door that led into the kitchen of the Palm Pavilion.

"Even though you think Lloyd is a jerk, the guys who surf think he's the greatest. Bruce surfs down at Castaway, too, and if he sees us talking to Lloyd—well, it will look very cool for us—and then Bruce will probably come over to talk to us, too," Chris explained.

"Why don't you just talk to him at work?" asked Liza. "He's here almost every day."

"Are you kidding?" said Chris as she took her time card from its metal slot and punched it into the slot above the wall clock. "Jannette Sansibar works here, too. Remember? She likes Bruce and she's so . . . I don't know . . . so blond."

"You're blond. I'm blond," said Sam. "So what?"

"I'm strawberry-blond. That doesn't count. Jannette is BLOND. You know what I mean. Besides, I can't talk to Bruce here. Mr. Parker thinks I'm always goofing off as it is. Parker would have a fit if he—" Chris cut herself short. A tall, pencil-thin man with sharp features and tight, tense lips had come up behind her. "Hello, Mr. Parker," she sputtered nervously.

"So, you think I have a bad temper, Miss Brown?" he asked.

"Ahhhhh, no sir, what I meant was . . ." Chris said, her voice shaking. "What I really was trying to say was . . ."

"She was saying you would fit into the United States Congress as a very distinguished senator if you didn't already fit into the hotel business so well," Sam jumped in.

Mr. Parker smoothed the sparse hair on his head across his bald spot. For a moment, he seemed pleased, then his stern demeanor returned. "I see," he said skeptically. He took Chris's time card from her hand, glanced at it, and then returned it to her.

6

"Would you care to read me the time on that card?"

"Uh, eight-thirty-three," said Chris.

"You are due here at eight-thirty. Eight-thirty-three is not eight-thirty," Mr. Parker said in the eerily calm voice he used whenever he was annoyed.

"Aw, come on, Mr. Parker," Liza said in her most charming voice. "It's only three minutes."

Mr. Parker's eyebrows shot up in an expression that was not promising. He took the card that Liza held in her hand. "Liza Velez," he read. "According to this card, you're not here at all."

"I was just about to punch it," said Liza with a small catch in her voice. Mr. Parker was the only person on earth who could make her lose her natural sassiness.

His piercing blue eyes studied her. Suddenly he looked startled as if he'd spotted something of unspeakable horror. "What, may I inquire, are those things?" he asked, pointing at Liza's pink high-tops.

"I have my white sneakers right in . . . this bag," said Liza, her voice trailing off. She didn't have a bag. She'd mistakenly left it on the kitchen table.

"Miss Velez, you know the dress code. You are to wear a polo shirt bearing the official Palm Pavilion logo, any shorts you choose and white — I repeat — *white* sneakers. *Clean* white sneakers."

"I didn't want them to get dirty on the ride over, that's why I kept them in a bag to change into here," Liza explained. "Only I left them in the basket of my bike. I'll be right back," she added quickly, turning toward the door.

"See that you hurry." He turned and stared at Chris's dingy sneakers. "And those, Miss Brown, do not fit my definition of — "

At that moment, the sharp sound of a man crying out in pain distracted him. The girls looked across the kitchen and saw the hotel's chef jumping up and down, waving his right hand wildly in the air.

"Idiot!" he screamed at the pale and trembling assistant chef at his side. "I told you to pound the veal, not my thumb!"

"I didn't expect you to . . . reach for the veal just then," the young man stammered nervously.

His excuse sent Chef Alleyne into a rage which he expressed loudly in his native tongue, French. In a moment, Mr. Parker was off, charging across the kitchen, waving his finger at the fat, red-haired chef. "Chef Alleyne! Please calm yourself!" he cried, as the rest of the kitchen staff tried to pretend they didn't notice the commotion.

Chef Alleyne thundered back at Mr. Parker, screaming something in French which the girls didn't understand. They seized the opportunity to make their escape through the kitchen door and out into the restaurant. "Whew! That was a close one," Chris sighed with relief.

"What are you going to do about your sneakers?" Sam asked Liza.

Liza twisted her face into a frustrated expression. "I can just see those sneakers sitting in the bag on the kitchen table. I was so worried about being late that I ran out without them. I'm going to have to stay out of Parker's way as best I can. Let's hope he has lots of crises today."

"Everything's a crisis to him," laughed Chris. "You were great when you said he would fit right into Congress, Sam. I thought I would die laughing."

"All this isn't funny, Chris," Sam snapped. Liza and Chris seemed to always take getting into trouble lightly. But it upset Sam. Whatever she did, she liked to do her best. It disturbed her not to give one hundred percent. "Parker could decide to fire us if he gets fed up. I like this job and I want to keep it."

"Sam, he's mad at us, not you. Relax," said Chris.

"He lumps the three of us together," Sam replied. "We're like the Three Musketeers to him."

"More like the Three Stooges," Liza chuckled.

"See what I mean! You guys don't take this job seriously," said Sam, exasperated.

"Oh, calm down, will you!" Liza told her. "I was just making a joke. Is that against the rules, too?"

"I'm sorry. I just hate getting into trouble all the time," Sam apologized.

"No problem," said Chris. "Next time Parker is mad at us — which should be any time in the next three minutes, with our luck — we'll pretend we don't know you."

Chris and Liza began walking through the restaurant, and out into the lobby. "Have you ever heard of anyone named Sam?" Chris asked her friend.

"No, can't say that I have," Liza replied.

"Me neither," Chris said.

"Never even heard the name before," said Liza.

Sam laughed and hurried to catch up with them. "Okay, okay! Wait up for me," she called.

The restaurant led out into the elegant pink-and-blue-tiled lobby. Round mahogany columns reached to the cathedral-style ceiling. Real palm trees and rubber plants flourished in their brass pots as they basked in the sun shining through the skylight overhead.

The girls were about to head toward the main desk to see if the assignment sheet had been posted yet, when Liza grabbed Chris and Sam by their arms. "Look! Look! What do you see?"

Sam's eyes darted around the lobby. She saw the antique furniture cushioned in soft greens and blues. She saw the open Parrot Lounge on the second floor balcony. She saw several guests waiting to check in or out. "I don't know," she said. "What do I see?"

"There!" Liza pointed to a man with long, straggly hair and faded jeans.

Chris gasped. "Cosmic Space Monsters!"

# Chapter Two

"You're right," said Sam. "That guy is the lead singer from Cosmic Space Monsters. What's his name, again?"

"Richie Rivers," Liza gushed. "Oh, I have to meet him. I *have* to, that's all there is to it."

Sam shot her a warning look. "Don't you remember how much trouble we almost got into when we sneaked into Harrison Springfield's room? We had to stand in his shower for over a half hour, waiting for a chance to escape!"

"Harrison Springfield was a famous actor. Richie Rivers wouldn't care," Liza argued. "He's a rocker." She headed out into the lobby.

Chris and Sam ran after her. "Where are you going?" Sam asked nervously.

"I'm getting his autograph," said Liza.

"You know we're not allowed to bother the famous guests," said Chris, hurrying alongside Liza.

"That's sin *numero uno* at the Palm Pavilion."

Liza stopped. "Okay, I know you're right. But if I met him, maybe we'd really hit it off. Then he'd see my star potential and let me join his band. It could happen."

"I thought you wanted to be a movie star, not a rock star," Sam reminded her.

"Rock stars get to be movie stars," said Liza. "Look at Cher. She started as a rock star and then she won an Academy Award. That could be me." She took a step away from them and tossed back her dark, silky hair. *"And the winner is . . . Liza!"* She looked at them, her eyes twinkling. "What do you think? Should I drop my last name? I'll be just *Liza.*"

"I think you should drop this whole idea of meeting Richie Rivers," said Sam.

"No, no, I can't," Liza muttered, as if she were already hatching a plan. "There's got to be a way to meet him without Parker finding out."

The girls watched as Richie Rivers gave his large snakeskin suitcase to the bellboy and disappeared down a long corridor leading to the elevators. Sam felt herself relax. Maybe if he was out of sight, Liza would forget about him. "The assignment sheet is going up," she said.

Near the front desk a petite oriental woman dressed in the crisp blue suit of the front desk staff posted a piece of paper on a bulletin board.

"Pray that Mrs. Chan put me on house service or

12

something," said Liza, as the girls headed over to read the sheet. When there weren't enough children to keep the baby sitters occupied, they were called upon to do other services and odd jobs around the hotel. House service was the job all the girls liked best. It was easy and they could see the insides of the fancy rooms. They even met some of the famous people when they delivered items from the hotel shops to them.

Liza read the sheet. "I don't believe it. I don't believe it," she fumed. "I'm stuck inside playing checkers with old Mr. Schwartz again! Isn't that guy ever going to leave? How come nobody else ever has to play with that old geezer?"

"I bet he requests you especially," Chris snickered.

"Yeah, because I don't say anything when he cheats—which is all the time," said Liza. "It isn't fair." Her eyes scanned the sheet. "You guys have regular baby-sitting assignments. Sunny has house service. I bet she'd trade with me."

"What have you got to trade?" asked a low, raspy voice behind Liza. She turned and saw Sunny, a short girl with long, red hair and too much eyeliner. She was one of the baby sitters at the Palm Pavilion whom the girls were friends with.

"I'll trade you house service for Mr. Schwartz," offered Liza.

"Sure. I'd rather sit around and play checkers

than be trotting up and down these halls all morning," Sunny answered.

"He has to win," Liza pointed out.

"No sweat. I don't know how to play checkers, anyway." Sunny shrugged.

"I don't think you should trade," Sam interrupted. "Or at least clear it with Mrs. Chan first."

"She won't find out," said Liza. "This will work out great."

Just then, Mrs. Chan looked up from her register at the front desk. "Oh, Samantha, the little boy you were supposed to sit for won't be getting here until tonight due to a delayed flight. I'm putting you on house service with Sunny for the next two hours."

"Oh, sure," Sam said. Her shoulders dropped in dismay. Now she would have to be part of Liza's plan. If Liza got caught, she'd surely be blamed right along with her. "Go wait by Mr. Halpern over at the far desk and he'll let you know if anyone needs anything," Mrs. Chan said.

Chris went off to collect the four-year-old girl she was assigned to watch. Sam and Liza walked across the lobby to a small desk with a sign that read "Customer Services." Mr. Halpern, a tall man with graying hair, smiled at them. "You my runners today?"

"Yep, no babies for the Pavilion baby sitters today," Liza chirped. She came up behind the man and looked over his shoulder at a large room plan

14

laid out on his desk. "This place is so huge," she said, looking down at the plan.

"Sure is," said Mr. Halpern. "Sit over there and I'll let you know when I need you."

Sam and Liza sat in the two straight-back chairs near Mr. Halpern's desk. "Guess what?" Liza whispered. "Mr. Halpern has every guest's name written in on that room plan. Richie Rivers is in room Sixteen-C. This is our chance to pay him a visit."

"What if he doesn't want anything from house service?" Sam asked.

Liza rolled her eyes. "Don't you get it? We just go to his room and say we made a mistake. Simple."

The phone on Mr. Halpern's desk rang. He answered, put the person on hold, and picked up another call. "I have an assignment for each of you," he said after he hung up. Liza was to bring a sewing kit from the gift shop to room 3-A. And Sam was sent to the Golf Pro shop to pick up a box of golf balls for a man in room 3-H.

"Meet me down at the end of this hall. We'll go to Richie Rivers' room together," Liza whispered excitedly.

"Liza, I don't think—" It was no use. Liza was hurrying off to the gift shop before Sam could finish her sentence.

This was really starting to bother Sam. If Chris and Liza wanted to flirt with disaster, that was their choice. But why did they have to keep dragging her into their schemes?

15

Sam headed for the Golf Pro shop at the far corner of the lobby. She pushed open the heavy glass door and immediately felt chilled by the air conditioning. Classical music played from an overhead speaker.

She'd never been inside the shop before. A rack of pastel-colored polo shirts with the Palm Pavilion Hotel crest lined one wall. In the center was a round rack with brightly colored pants and shorts. Sam could never get used to the way some golfers dressed, with their plain tops and bright pants. The other day she'd seen a distinguished-looking man with silvery hair wearing electric green-and-orange plaid pants.

Along the other wall were golf clubs of different shapes and sizes. A leather golf bag hung from the ceiling in the corner. The glass counter at the far end of the store featured books about golfing, golf tees, balls, handkerchiefs and other odds and ends.

Behind the counter, waiting on a customer, was a beautiful girl. Her white-blonde hair fell evenly to her chin. A golden tan set off her porcelain-blue eyes. Sam had never seen her before, which was strange since Bonita Beach was a small town with only one school. Even though the girl looked a couple of years older than Sam, she should have at least seen her in school.

"Can I help you?" the girl asked, catching sight of Sam.

16

"I need golf balls for some guy in room Three-H," she said.

The girl got the balls from the case and wrote up a sales receipt, marking the room number in the top right corner. She tucked her hair behind one ear and the sparkle from a pair of small diamond earrings caught Sam's eye. "Anything else?" she asked pleasantly.

Sam shook her head. "Aren't you freezing in here?" she asked, rubbing the goose bumps on her arms.

"No," said the girl. "You get used to it."

Sam looked around. It was like a different world inside the shop—everything was very quiet and peaceful. It seemed to be isolated from all the bustling activity of the hotel. "Do you like working here?" Sam asked.

The girl shrugged. "It gets a little dull. But it's the only thing my father would let me do. He didn't want me to work, but I couldn't bear another summer of sitting around the pool. Besides, I want to earn some money on my own."

"I don't blame you," Sam smiled. Judging from the girl's elegant looks, Sam had thought she might be snobbish. But she didn't seem that way at all. "Well, so long," Sam said. "Nice talking to you."

"Bye," said the girl with a quick smile. "Don't forget to give one copy of the sales slip to the front desk so they can bill Three-H."

"I won't." Sam left the shop and found Liza waiting for her at the end of the hall.

"Ready?" she asked brightly.

"I'm not going with you," Sam stated flatly.

"Yes you are. You never let me down," Liza replied, pulling her toward the elevators. "You said you wouldn't go to Harrison Springfield's room and you did."

"And I learned my lesson from it," Sam protested. She had to smile, despite her concern. One of the things she liked about Liza was her adventurous spirit. She never seemed afraid to do anything daring.

Liza pulled Sam into the express elevator that ran to the top floors where the fancy suites were located. There were only three suites on each floor. Sam pressed button sixteen. Silently, the elevator car rose. It went directly to the seventeenth floor without a stop.

"Hey, it just passed sixteen!" Liza cried, looking up at the light. "The elevators in this hotel are always screwy."

"Too bad," Sam said quickly. "Might as well press the down button and forget the whole thing."

"No way," said Liza as the doors opened. "We just take the fire stairs down and — " Liza was stopped by the sight of a very tall man with a blond crew cut wearing a light blue suit. He had a walkie-talkie in one hand. He looked at Sam and Liza with intense blue eyes.

18

"What's your business here, ladies?" he asked with a straight face.

"Ummm . . . delivering stuff, to, uh . . . another room downstairs," Liza stammered, flustered.

"What room would that be?" asked the man.

Sam and Liza looked at one another guiltily. What room should they say? "One on the sixteenth floor," Sam finally answered. "But the elevator didn't stop there." She chuckled nervously. "These elevators are always messing up. You might have noticed — "

"May I see those sales tickets?" the man cut her off. As he reached for them, Sam saw that he had a gun holstered under his jacket. From the expression on her face, Sam knew that Liza had seen it, too. With trembling hands they handed the man their sales tickets.

"These are for the third floor," he noted.

"Are they?" said Liza, acting surprised. "Let me see those. How could we have made such a mistake?" She reached for the sales tickets but the man didn't hand them back to her. Instead, he pointed toward the elevator and stepped in with them. "This is Blue Man seventeen," he spoke into his walkie-talkie. "I need a replacement. Taking down two employees found attempting entry to ambassador's room."

He pressed the "down" button and the door closed. *Ambassador's room!* thought Sam. *Oh, no!*

# Chapter Three

"What is going on here?!" cried Mr. Parker, dashing across the lobby toward them.

"I caught these two on floor seventeen," said the man. Sam could feel herself blushing with embarrassment as all eyes in the lobby turned toward them.

Mr. Parker rolled his eyes. "And did they appear to be dangerous to you?"

It was the man's turn to look embarrassed. "They were supposed to be on the third floor," he said, handing Mr. Parker the sales tickets. "And I thought they might not be real hotel staff because of the way that one is dressed." As he spoke, he pointed down at Liza's pink sneakers.

Mr. Parker gazed down at Liza's feet and then breathed deeply in an attempt to calm himself. "How did this happen, ladies?" he asked sternly.

"Ummmmm . . . we stepped onto the express

elevator by mistake," said Sam.

"I see," said Mr. Parker, sounding satisfied. "That's an easy mistake to — "

Just then, old Mr. Schwartz hobbled up to them. His cane clattered across the floor. "That's her," the bony old man shouted, pointing a gnarled finger at Liza. "She's the one I always play checkers with. I don't want that other red-haired girl. I specifically asked for *her*."

"She will be right with you, I assure you," Mr. Parker told the old man.

Mr. Schwartz nodded grouchily and turned back toward his table. "I'm paying good money to stay here. I want what I want when I want it," he mumbled as he left.

Liza spoke up in a small voice. "I traded with Sunny for house service," she said.

"Any particular reason why?" Mr. Parker asked casually.

"I was hoping that the guy from Cosmic Space Monsters would order something so I could bring it to his room," Liza confessed.

"Do I understand you correctly?" asked Mr. Parker, scratching the side of his cheek. "You were under the impression that we have a guest from outer space here at the hotel and you were hoping to contact him?"

"No, no. He's from the rock band, Cosmic Space Monsters," Liza explained.

"Uh-huh. How fascinating." Mr. Parker turned to

21

the security guard. "And you? You were under the impression that these two were . . . what? Enemy agents? Spies?"

"You must remember, Mr. Parker," the man protested, "that when you hired the Blue Man Security Force, you said to report any, I repeat *any*, suspicious looking persons who were seen lurking near the ambassador from India."

"Yes, but use some common sense next time, will you?!" Mr. Parker exploded.

"This is an international situation," said the guard. "Children are often deployed by unfriendly forces in perpetrating sabotage and other — "

"Fine, fine," said Mr. Parker impatiently. "Go man your post. I want Ambassador Rama, his wife and their ten children to have a pleasant, tranquil vacation. That's the only reason I hired your company."

"That's what they're going to have," said the man. He turned and headed back to the elevators.

Mr. Parker turned back to Liza, a fierce look on his face. "Now please go play checkers with Mr. Schwartz and keep those . . . those *pink* things tucked under the table. If I ever see them here again, I will send you home immediately."

"Sure, okay. Sorry, Mr. Parker," said Liza, backing away.

"Go play checkers!" Mr. Parker barked. Liza handed Sam the sewing kit and scampered across the lobby toward Mr. Schwartz. Mr. Parker then leaned closer to Sam and said, "And you had better be careful about letting your friends pull you into their shenanigans. You are here to work. Understood?"

"Yes, sir. Understood," said Sam obediently.

Mr. Parker took off toward the front desk. Sam remembered that the man in 3-H still hadn't gotten his golf balls. And the person in 3-A needed the sewing kit. She took the elevator up and delivered both items.

The house service desk was busy for the rest of the morning. Sam got another call to pick up golf tees and deliver them. This time, when she went into the Pro Shop, the salesgirl she'd seen earlier was walking out the door, a bag of golf clubs slung over her shoulder.

"Boy, they have you delivering stuff, too?" said Sam as she walked in. She noticed that the girl's pink shorts had the kind of sharp creases that came from dry cleaning. A delicate gold watch gleamed on her wrist.

The girl smiled. "No, I'm off now. I thought I'd play a few holes of golf before going home."

"You play golf?" said Sam, impressed. "I never knew a girl who played golf."

"Dad taught me to play several years ago when we went up to Bermuda for vacation. It's a terrific game. You don't play?"

"No, but I've always wanted to learn," Sam replied. She didn't know why she'd said that. Golf was just about the only sport that didn't appeal to her. But there was something special about this girl. And golf suddenly seemed like a very sophisticated game.

"My name is Trisha Royce, by the way," the girl introduced herself, extending her hand.

"Samantha O'Neill." Sam offered her hand. It felt odd, though, since the only other time she'd shaken hands with anyone was when she graduated from the eighth grade last month. Then she'd shaken the principal's hand when he gave her the diploma. It felt strange, but very grown-up.

"Would you like to have a golf lesson tomorrow? I'd be glad to show you the basics," said Trisha.

Sam was thrilled. "That would be great! I get done with work at two."

"So do I. Perfect. It's a little hot then, but we won't play for too long. See you tomorrow." Trisha smiled at Sam and cut across the lobby, out toward the golf course.

Sam got the golf tees and delivered them. All the while she imagined herself playing golf with Trisha. What a nice person Trisha was to offer golf lessons to someone she hardly knew! Sam hoped she wouldn't make a fool of herself. But she realized that she was just a bit nervous. She had always had a natural strength and agility that made sports easy and fun for her.

After work, Sam met up with Liza and Chris in front of the hotel. They rode home together, as usual. At the corner of Vine and Grove Streets, Sam turned off toward home.

"Don't worry, Sam, tomorrow will be better," Liza assured her. "I'm sorry about getting you into trouble."

"It's okay," Sam grumbled.

"This time I wasn't involved, thank goodness," said Chris. "From now on the Palm Pavilion baby sitters will be pictures of perfection. Does that make you feel better, Sam?"

A small laugh escaped from Sam. "All right, already. You make me sound like a goody-goody. I want to do a good job. That's just how I am."

"You're absolutely right. Chris and I take too many chances. But no more. You'll never have to worry about us again," said Liza. She smiled mischievously. "When I saw that guy's gun I thought we were history."

"Me, too," Sam agreed. "I wonder if we'll get to see that Indian ambassador."

"If this guy really has ten kids, we're sure to see at least one of them!" commented Chris.

"Not if they have their own nanny," Liza pointed out.

"I guess we'll find out tomorrow," Sam laughed. She waved good-bye to her friends and rode toward her house. She turned up a dirt driveway, and passed a large, white stucco house. Her house was the smaller white one on the back plot of land. The Jamesons lived in the larger stucco house only

25

during the winter. They had just left for the summer and Sam was thrilled that her family could use both yards now, since there was no fence dividing them.

She stopped her bike in front of the house. Her sister Greta's old blue car stood behind a van which had the words *Captain Dan's Snorkeling Tours* emblazoned on its side in a swirling hot-pink script. Sam never understood why her father had let Greta paint the sign for him. Personally, she thought it looked tacky and very unprofessional. Her father had laughed and said he thought it was "unusual and eye-catching."

Sam leaned her bike against the front porch and climbed the steps. When she opened the front door, a strange sight greeted her. Her mother had five bowls of dried dog food lined up across the living room floor, and she was kneeling in front of them.

"Mom!" Sam cried. "What are you doing?"

# Chapter Four

Mrs. O'Neill looked up and blew a strand of curly red hair from her face. "This must be a strange sight!" she laughed. "I'm waiting for Trevor to come out of the kitchen." Her mother clapped her hands. "Come on, good boy. Come on. Just two more bowls to go."

A large black Labrador retriever stuck his head out of the kitchen doorway. "What's going on, Mom?" Sam asked, plunking down onto the large flowered couch.

Mrs. O'Neill leaned back on her heels. "Well, you know I've started selling Chompy Pet pet food. These are the five different kinds of dog food we sell. I'm trying to get Trevor's opinion. He hated the liver flavor, obviously, because he ran out of the room whimpering just now."

Sam ruffled the smooth hair between Trevor's ears. "Poor boy," she laughed.

"Come on, Trevor," Mrs. O'Neill coaxed. "Try the Beef Banquet." She pushed the bowl forward. Trevor sniffed it and then looked back at Sam with pitiful eyes.

"I think that's a 'no,' Mom," Sam observed.

"Well, I just don't know," her mother said. "They told me animals love this food so much it practically sells itself."

"They told you that about the Bluebell House Cleaners, too," Sam recalled. Her mother was always starting new money-making ventures that never seemed to work out. Their garage was now stocked with at least a year's supply of Bluebell floor polish, rug shampoo, toilet cleaner, and other cleaning items her mother had been unable to sell.

"We'll have the cleanest house in Bonita Beach," her father had said on the day Mrs. O'Neill turned in her Bluebell cap that she wore door-to-door. But they didn't. For the most part the products had remained in the garage. Mrs. O'Neill was not a fussy housekeeper. She was too busy with her various business ideas to use much Bluebell disinfectant scrub.

Then there was the time she tried selling magazine subscriptions over the phone. And there was the fiasco when she tried to run a bakery from their house. There were several large bags of flour next to the Bluebell products to remind everyone of *that* doomed venture. It seemed that everything

Mrs. O'Neill baked resembled a paperweight more than it did anything edible.

Sam could have listed a number of other ideas that hadn't worked out for her mother. "Why don't you just go get a job?" she'd asked.

"What? And leave you kids!" her mother had cried, horrified at the idea.

"Greta's seventeen and I'm fourteen," she'd protested.

"You're not so old that you don't need your mother anymore," she had replied.

"How's it going?" Mr. O'Neill asked, stepping into the living room from the back bedroom.

"I give up!" sighed her mother, picking up the bowl of Beef Banquet and putting it on the table. "I'm not going to even try the Seafood Delight on him. Who ever heard of a dog liking fish? He hasn't liked one of these." Mrs. O'Neill slumped off into the kitchen with the remaining bowls of Chompy Pet cradled in her arms.

Mr. O'Neill slapped his small pot belly. That was Trevor's signal to jump up and lick Mr. O'Neill's face. "Trevor's kind of an oddball," he chuckled as the dog laid juicy slurps onto his cheek. "You can't judge sane dogs by him. I'm sure other dogs will lap this stuff up."

*Why do you encourage her?* Sam wanted to ask. No matter what her mother did, her father thought it was a great idea — until it failed. Then he turned around and said it wasn't Mrs.

O'Neill's fault, the product just wasn't any good and once she found the right one, she'd do very well.

Mr. O'Neill went to the living room table and put on a white captain's hat with a blue peak. It looked odd with his Hawaiian shirt patterned with orange flying fish leaping the waves. "Why do you always have to wear that captain's hat?" Sam asked, irritated.

"Because I'm Captain Dan. People expect me to look like a captain when I take them out on my boat."

"It makes you look like a geek," Sam mumbled.

"You think it makes me look Greek?"

"I didn't say Greek. I said — "

"I know what you said," her father cut her off. "Some people have no taste." He smiled at her and headed for the door. "Oh, hello there," he greeted Lloyd and Greta, who were coming into the living room from outside.

"Hi, Mr. O., Mrs. O.," said Lloyd, tossing his long, white-blond bangs from his eyes. Of all Lloyd's annoying habits, the one that bothered Sam the most was the way Lloyd flipped his hair back every five minutes. Sam couldn't imagine what Greta saw in him. Sure, he had a gorgeous tan and big muscles. But to Sam, he never sounded intelligent. But, then, Sam figured, maybe he and Greta were a good match in the brains department.

"The waves were really breaking down at the

Castaway," Greta gushed as she hopped into the room. She had the same red hair as their mother, but she'd bleached it platinum blond and now red roots were showing.

"That reminds me, Lloyd," said Sam, getting up from the couch. "I have this really embarrassing favor to ask. Could my friends come with me to watch you surf sometime?"

"It's a free beach," said Lloyd, popping a few pieces of Beef Banquet into his mouth. "Hey, these are good," he said. "Better than those little cheese goldfish."

"Lloyd . . ." said Sam in a flat tone.

Lloyd threw another handful into his mouth. "Yeah?"

"That's dog food you're eating."

A spray of Chompy Pet flew out of Lloyd's mouth. Greta grabbed Sam's arm. "Sam! I don't believe you let him eat that!"

Sam stifled a smile. "I told him it was dog food!"

Lloyd wiped his mouth. "Actually, it wasn't bad, until you told me what it was."

"Hey, Mom!" Sam called into the kitchen. "There's hope. Lloyd liked the Beef Banquet." She turned to Lloyd. "Mom has four other flavors you might like to sample."

"Sam, you're such a little brat," shouted Greta.

"Oh, can it, Greta," Sam snapped. "So, Lloyd, if we come down and watch you, would you just act like you know us?"

"I do know you," Lloyd pointed out.

"I know, but you have to act like you *like* us. You see, my friend Chris likes a boy who thinks you're great. So, if he sees that you know us, he'll think we're cool," Sam explained calmly, "and like us, too."

"Huh?" said Greta grouchily. "I don't see why Lloyd should do you any favors after you let him eat dog food."

"It wasn't my idea. Chris asked me to ask."

"Then Chris should ask Lloyd herself." Before Sam could reply, Mrs. O'Neill came to the kitchen doorway. "Lloyd, I realize it was an accident, but did you really like the Beef Banquet?"

"It was kind of cool," Lloyd told her. "It had a sort of beef jerky taste with almost a hint of curry."

"Do dogs like the taste of curry?" asked Greta.

"Trevor certainly didn't," said Mrs. O'Neill. "Maybe that's the problem. I should write to the company and tell them."

"I'm not exactly sure it was curry, though," said Lloyd.

Sam rolled her eyes and shook her head. It seemed to her that she lived in the only house in the world where this kind of conversation could possibly take place.

She left them discussing the taste of Chompy Pet and climbed the narrow stairs to the dormer bedroom she shared with Greta. Inside, she stepped over the red ribbon she'd laid across the floor to separate her side of the room from Greta's. It wasn't that she disliked Greta so much, but her sister was a slob. Her side of the room looked like someone had planted a small bomb — which had exploded and tossed all her belongings onto the floor, the chair and even the windowsill.

In contrast, Sam's side was neat. Her bed was made, her clothes were put away. It was her haven of order in this chaotic household.

She pulled on the overhead fan and laid down on top of her flowered bedspread. It had been a busy day and she realized she was tired. She thought about the man in the blue suit with the gun under his jacket. She remembered Mr. Parker's red face as he yelled at them.

Then she thought about Trisha Royce, the girl she had met at the Pro Shop. She wondered what Trisha was doing right now. What did *her* house look like? What was *her* family like? One thing was for sure: They weren't in the living room discussing the flavor of dog food.

# Chapter Five

"You wanted to see the ambassador's kids!" said Chris. "Well, you got your wish."

Chris, Liza, and Sam had been put in charge of the seven youngest of the Indian ambassador's ten children. The oldest one in their care was eleven-year-old Naima. The youngest was three-year-old Nahib. In the middle were children aged four, five, seven, eight and nine.

"We have almost enough kids for a baseball team," laughed Sam as the kids followed them to one of the hotel's three pools.

"I hope you are making a joke. I am not very good at baseball," said seven-year-old Ismail shyly. "My little brother Kashi is a slugger. But me, not so good neither."

"That's okay," said Sam, walking alongside him. "I'm not so good at baseball, myself. Today we're just going to swim around in the pool and have a good time."

They stopped when they reached the kidney-shaped pool nearest the beach. They had picked it because it was only five feet at its deepest end, and at least half of it was only three feet deep. "This is a baby pool," said eleven-year-old Naima. "I want to go to the beach."

"Me, too," agreed nine-year-old Rekha. "I am an excellent swimmer."

"We have to stay together," said Liza. "It's too dangerous down at the beach. We can't keep our eyes on all of you."

"I do not need someone watching over me," Naima insisted. "I am much too old for to have babysitting."

"Then you can help us look after your brothers and sisters," said Chris. "Come on. Everyone into the pool."

Chris was glad that they were staying in this pool. Unlike Rekha, she was not an excellent swimmer. She would be looking after Rekha, Naima and eight-year-old Dira, while Liza looked after Kashi and Ismail. Sam had little Nahib and Salu. They had divided the kids this way, reasoning that the bigger girls were least likely to get into trouble in the water. Although there was a lifeguard on duty, the kids were the girls' special responsibility.

Chris sat at the five-foot end of the pool and let her feet dangle in the water. The little girls got themselves kickboards and began to flutter-kick back and forth. They were good swimmers and Chris was happy for the chance to sit in the sun and relax as they amused themselves.

Chris's favorite thing in the world, outside of double chocolate-chip ice cream and Bruce Johnson, was TV trivia. She just loved old TV shows. As the sun beat down on her, Chris began to daydream that she was a member of the "Gilligan's Island" crew. And so was Bruce. She pictured them together, sitting on the beach of the deserted island in the moonlight. Somehow they had managed to find a container of double chocolate-chip ice cream. Bruce was feeding it to her as the waves lapped at their feet.

"Hi," said a voice beside her. Immediately Chris's heart began pounding. She knew it was Bruce Johnson.

She pulled close the big shirt she wore over her one-piece aqua bathing suit. "Hi," she answered, looking up at him and smiling. *Oh, why couldn't I have lost that ten pounds already?* she wondered miserably. *And why do I have to be wearing my least-favorite bathing suit?*

"Are you off-duty?" he asked.

Chris nodded with her chin toward the three girls in the pool. "No, I'm baby-sitting," she said.

Bruce shielded his eyes from the sun and looked into the pool. "Are those the ambassador's kids?" Chris nodded. "That Parker is crazy," laughed

Bruce. "Can you believe he hired all those guards to protect the guy? He's just an ambassador. He's not the president or anything."

Chris loved the fact that Bruce had stopped to talk to her like this. It meant he thought of her as a friend. That was a step in the right direction, anyway. Before this hotel job she had just been some kid in the lower grades whom he barely knew was alive. Working at the hotel together had given them something in common.

"Mr. Parker had a fit the other day when my friends got too close to the ambassador's room," Chris said. "They weren't even looking for the ambassador. Liza wanted to meet Richie Rivers from the Cosmic Space Monsters."

"I saw him checking out this morning," said Bruce.

"He checked out!" cried Chris. "Liza will have a fit when she finds out she missed him. I'm glad he left, though. I know Liza would have tried again to meet him, and if Parker had caught her, he would've totally lost his cool."

"He's always flipping his lid over something or other," said Bruce. "The other day he told me I didn't stack the beach chairs correctly. I mean, come on, how picky can you get?"

Chris laughed. Then she worried that maybe she'd laughed too loudly and put a serious expression back on her face. "Done much surfing lately?" she asked, trying to sound casual.

"Yeah, Castaway has been great. The other day I caught a wave and it didn't seem like it was ever going to end. Usually, you only get to ride for about — "

"Excuse me," Chris interrupted him. She had glanced back at the pool. The girls were gone!

She jumped to her feet. "Did you see where those kids went?" she asked Bruce.

"You mean they're gone?" he asked. Both of them looked at the other end of the pool. The girls weren't there, either. "Okay, you know they didn't drown. They're just not here," he said. "They couldn't have gone far."

Chris and Bruce looked in all directions. "There they are," he said, pointing out toward the beach. The three girls were running toward the water, their red kickboards held over their heads like surfboards.

To make matters worse, Mr. Parker suddenly appeared, walking toward them from the hotel. "Oh, no," Chris moaned. "What am I going to do?"

"I'll distract him while you go round the kids up," said Bruce.

"Okay. Thanks." Chris ran toward the beach. Even in her panic, she couldn't help admiring Bruce's take-charge manner. And now he was going out of his way to help her. Maybe he was starting to like her, after all!

She raced down to the shore. By the time she got there, the girls were kicking their way out toward a raft anchored about ten yards from shore. "Girls!" she shouted. "Naima, Rekha, Dira!"

The girls heard her and looked back for a few seconds. Chris saw them glance at one another, but they had obviously decided to ignore her. They kept swimming toward the raft.

She kicked off her sandals and waded into the surf. A small wave hit her stomach and knocked her back a few steps. "Girls!" she shouted again. This time they didn't even turn around. Chris knew she wasn't a strong enough swimmer to go out there and round them up.

*What should I do now?* she wondered. *I could go to the lifeguard and ask her to go get them. But that would probably turn into a major commotion. Mr. Parker would be sure to hear about it. I have to think of something — and fast.* Then it came to her: Sam! She was a great swimmer. Chris raced back toward the pool. She looked around and saw that Bruce was talking to Mr. Parker. They were standing by a stack of beach chairs and Mr. Parker was demonstrating how to stack them. Chris knew that wouldn't last much longer.

"Sam! Sam!" Chris called breathlessly from the pool's edge.

Sam looked up. She had been playing ball in the shallow water with Nahib and Salu. "What's the matter, Chris?" she asked.

In a frantic tone, Chris explained the situation. "So you have to go out there and bring them back," she concluded. Chris saw Sam check around the pool area for Mr. Parker. "Bruce is distracting him," she told Sam.

"Everything okay?" called Liza from the middle of the pool.

"Not really," moaned Chris miserably.

Sam threw her the ball. "Don't take your eyes off these two, okay?" she said, clearly annoyed. She climbed out of the pool. "I don't believe this," Chris heard her grumble as she hurried off down to the beach.

# *Chapter Six*

Sam swam out toward the girls on the raft. "Come on back, girls," she called, treading water in front of them.

"We like it here," said Trina. "It's much better than that little pool. At home we have a gigantic pool all to ourselves. We never get to go to the beach, though."

Sam couldn't really blame them. She liked the beach much better herself. "I'll make a deal with you!" she called. "If you come in now, we'll take you to the beach tomorrow. I have to get permission, though. If I take you without permission I'll get into trouble."

The girls looked at one another. "You are a big person. How can you get into trouble?" asked Dira.

"Believe me, I'm not that big. I can get into lots of trouble if you don't come in."

"Oh," said Naima. "We did not know this. Sorry."

41

With three little splashes, the girls dropped into the water with their kickboards. Sam swam alongside them until they reached the shore.

When they walked up toward the pool, Sam's heart sank. There was Mr. Parker standing by the edge of the pool talking to Liza and Chris. The rest of the ambassador's kids stood beside them, dripping wet. From the look on Mr. Parker's face, Sam could tell he was not at all pleased.

"There you are," he said when she approached. "Your friends here tell me you took these children for a little swim in the ocean. Is that so?"

"They . . . ummm . . . they asked to go," stammered Sam, "and I didn't think there would be any harm in it. I — "

"You know there are rules about taking children onto the beach without first obtaining permission from the parents," he scolded. "And you know whose children these are. We do not want any incidents during his stay!"

"I'm sorry, I didn't realize — " Sam continued.

"It was my fault," Chris spoke up. "I let them get away from me and I asked Sam to bring them back because she's a better swimmer."

Mr. Parker's face went red with anger. "You let them . . . they were in the water . . . they got away." He took one of his famous deep breaths to calm himself.

"Miss O'Neill," he said slowly. "When I hired you three, I thought you were the sensible one of the group. But I'm beginning to doubt that judgement. In fact, I'm starting to think you are the ringleader!"

"It really wasn't her fault," Liza insisted.

Mr. Parker glared menacingly at her. "Does Miss O'Neill have a brain? Or have you taken possession of it?"

"No, she has a brain. I only meant — " Liza began.

"Then I think she can decide for herself what she should and should not do!" he snapped. "Please," he continued, "the waiters are threatening to strike, Chef Alleyne is in one of his moods, and the ice machine on the first floor is overheating and pumping torrents of water onto the carpeting, even as we speak. Therefore, I implore you, no, I beg of you — KEEP YOUR EYES ON THESE KIDS!"

"Yes, sir," the girls said at once. Mr. Parker turned and headed back to the hotel at his usual brisk pace.

"I'm really sorry, Sam," said Chris.

"How could you let that happen!" Sam exploded. "When you're guarding someone in the pool you're not supposed to take your eyes off them for a second."

"There is a lifeguard on duty," Chris defended herself. "I just looked away for a minute."

"It was more than a minute. I saw you talking to Bruce."

"What were you doing looking at me?" Chris shot

back. "How come *you* weren't staring at the kids every second?"

"Come on, you two. Calm down," Liza cut in. "You're both just upset because Parker yelled at us. He'll get over it. He hasn't fired us yet."

"*Yet*," Sam echoed Liza.

"I want to go back into the pool," said Ismail.

"All right, everyone, back in the pool," said Liza brightly. Chris and Sam went back to opposite ends of the pool. Sam tried not to be angry, but she couldn't help it. She was tired of taking the heat for her friends' irresponsible acts.

The rest of the baby-sitting session went by without any problems. At two o'clock, all seven of the kids were assembled on the back deck of the hotel. A small, dark woman in a sari emerged from the back entrance. The thin, purple-print fabric of her outfit wafted gently in the breeze. A small diamond glistened from the corner of her nose. She smiled and nodded at Sam, Chris and Liza. "Were my children well-behaved?" she asked in a soft, warm voice.

Rekha and Naima looked at Chris with worried expressions. "They were great," Chris said cheerfully.

"I am pleased," said the ambassador's wife. With a flowing wave of her hand, she beckoned the children to follow her into the hotel.

"Boy, she sure has them under control," Sam said in admiration.

"I love her outfit. It's totally cool," Liza commented.

"Speaking of totally cool, I'm roasting. Let's punch out and get out of here," said Chris.

"Good idea," Liza agreed, stepping into her shorts. "Why don't we go down to Castaway? Today would be a good day for our plan with Lloyd."

"Yeah," Chris agreed. "Did you see how Bruce covered for me? What do you think it means?"

Liza re-did the elastic on her long, dark ponytail. " I think he definitely likes you, but I'm not sure how much. We'll be able to tell better this afternoon. Lloyd said it was okay, right, Sam?"

"He said it would be fine, but I can't go today," Sam answered. "You can talk to Lloyd without me."

"No we can't! Lloyd hardly knows us!" Chris cried. "Why can't you come?"

"I made a date to go play golf with a girl I met in the Pro Shop the other day," Sam told them. She was surprised at how small and apologetic her voice sounded. Why did she feel bad? It was a free country. She was allowed to have friends besides Liza and Chris.

Liza and Chris stood looking at her with stunned expressions. "You told us just the other day that you can't play golf," Liza challenged.

"I know. Trisha is going to teach me."

"You mean you're playing with that snobby blonde girl from the golf store?" Chris asked.

"Not the golf store, the Pro Shop," Sam corrected her.

"Whatever," Chris said impatiently.

"And how do you know she's a snob?" said Sam, tying her sneakers. "Have you ever spoken to her?"

"No," Chris admitted, "but you can tell by the way she walks." She lifted her chin and stuck out her hips. She began walking in an exaggerated fashion, wiggling her hips and waving her arms back and forth at her side.

"She does not walk like that!" Sam said irritably.

"Anyway, you promised to go to Castaway with us," said Liza.

"I didn't promise. You just assumed I was going," Sam argued.

Chris's lower lip protruded in a pout. "I was so psyched about this that I hardly slept last night. I even got up at three in the morning and ironed a pair of shorts."

"See, Sam," said Liza. "She's so demented over this that she's ironing! In the middle of the night! You *have* to come."

"All right, already," sighed Sam. "I'll be home by four. The guys surf until it's almost dark. We'll have plenty of time."

Chris planted a big kiss on Sam's cheek. "Thank you! Thank you! Thank you!" she said happily.

"Okay!" Sam smiled. They walked together through the lobby to the kitchen. When they reached the time clock, Trisha was already there, punching out.

"Ready to go?" she asked Sam with a smile. "I have my clubs back in the shop. We can share them, for the time being."

"Great!" Sam said. "These are my friends Liza and Chris." She waited to see how they would react to Trisha when she extended her hand to shake theirs — but she never did. She smiled weakly and nodded. Liza and Chris mirrored her expression, smiling and nodding back halfheartedly.

"I'll meet you in front of the shop in five," said Trisha, tossing her silky blond hair away from her face. "You're going to love the game. I just know it." Trisha smiled again at Chris and Liza and then hurried out of the kitchen.

"She's certainly solid, isn't she," observed Liza.

"I think she has a great figure," Sam said, punching her card.

"Didn't you see the muscles on her arms and legs?" said Chris.

Sam wanted to say that it was better to have extra muscle than flab, but she didn't want to hurt Chris's feelings. "I think a little muscle looks good on a girl," she said instead.

Chris shrugged. "Maybe."

"I'll see you at four," Sam said.

"You forgot something," said Liza. "Our bikes are chained together. You would have left us out there with no way to get home while you were teeing off."

47

"Okay," said Sam, digging in her pocket for the key. "You act like I did it on purpose." She handed Liza the key to the chain. "When you're done, lock mine back up and leave the key tucked under the seat."

"Don't forget to meet us at four," Chris reminded her.

"I won't," said Sam. She left them standing by the time clock. It felt strange not to be leaving the hotel together. Once again, she had the strangely disturbing feeling of being disloyal to them. Was it such a crime to do something with someone else once in a while?

She knew there was more to it. She didn't want to admit it, but they had been annoying her lately. *Could it be that I'm outgrowing my old friends? No — that can't be it.* She'd been best friends with Liza and Chris since elementary school.

Sam left the kitchen and passed through the restaurant where a few lunch customers still lingered. The busboys were already setting up for the dinner crowd. She saw Trisha waiting for her in the lobby by the Pro Shop. She'd pushed her hair back with a black cloth headband. Sam looked at her tanned, lean figure. Trisha did have muscular arms, as Chris had said, but they weren't bulky or manly. She looked trim, like a real athlete. Sam realized that Trisha was everything she herself dreamed of being someday — cool, elegant, confident and athletic.

Trisha's face brightened when she caught sight of Sam. "Come on," she said. "I'm going to make a world-class golfer out of you!"

# *Chapter Seven*

Trisha stopped at the edge of the grass and tied a white sun visor around her head. "You're going to have to get one of these and a good pair of sunglasses," she said, fixing the bow of the visor strap. Sam had never seen a visor that was so feminine and soft. It looked perfect with Trisha's straight, shiny hair.

Sam stepped out onto the golf course behind Trisha. "This is a nine-hole, par thirty-five championship course," Trisha said. Sam nodded, as if Trisha's words made sense to her. Trisha pulled a golf club from her white leather golf bag. "Try a wooden club to start with," she advised.

Trisha and Sam went to the tee-off area and Trisha set the ball on a tee. Then she showed Sam how to stand. "Feet apart, knees slightly bent." The position felt awkward to Sam. "Drop your shoulders, you're too tense," Trisha coached.

The first two times she tried, Sam didn't connect with the golf ball at all. "Maybe golf just isn't my sport," she said, embarrassed.

"Hang in there," said Trisha. "You'll get it." The third time, when Sam did hit the ball, it went high into the air and nowhere near the flag which marked the hole she was aiming for. "At least you hit it that time," Trisha encouraged her. "Here, watch me."

Sam handed her the club. Trisha positioned herself in front of the ball and swung. The ball traveled in a straight line and fell halfway between the tee and the hole.

"Do you play a lot?" Sam asked as they walked toward the ball.

"Every chance I get," Trisha answered. "I'd love to turn pro someday, but Daddy won't hear of it. We fight about it all the time."

"Why does he object?" asked Sam.

Trisha sighed. "He says playing sports for money is tacky. He thinks it would embarrass the family or something like that. He's so old-fashioned."

"I thought golf was a, you know, classy kind of sport," said Sam. "It's not like you want to play pro football or something. And even then, what's tacky about earning that much money?"

Trisha laughed lightly. "My family already *has* that much money. I wouldn't be doing it for the money, anyway, I'd do it for the challenge."

"Well, sure, of course," said Sam, suddenly feeling

tacky herself. She often fantasized about being a professional sportswoman, maybe a tennis star. The challenge was a big part of it — but so was the money. Sam saw sports as the only possible way she would ever earn a lot of money. It wasn't that she was so materialistic, but, just as Liza dreamed of being a movie star and other girls dreamed of being rock stars or models, Sam wanted to be a champion athlete on the cover of a magazine. Even when she daydreamed about winning the Olympics, money and fame were involved. First she'd picture them putting the gold medal around her neck, then she saw herself on TV, endorsing healthy cereals. . . .

"You could always give the money to charity," Sam suggested.

"You're brilliant," said Trisha, flashing Sam a dazzling smile. "I'm going to mention that to Daddy tonight. He can't possibly object to charity." She patted Sam on the back. "I could tell you had brains the first minute I saw you."

Trisha's words made Sam smile. "You could? How?"

Trisha put the wooden club back into her bag and pulled out a metal one. "You have an intelligent face," she said, lining up another shot. Again, she swung, throwing her whole body into the shot. The ball landed within inches of the flag.

Sam noticed that the grass under their feet was shorter and more yellowish. "Now we're on the green," said Trisha, changing clubs again.

"What's that?" Sam asked.

"This grass is specially developed for the area near the hole. I'll take the flag out. You try to sink it," she said, handing Sam the golf club.

Sam walked to the ball and tapped it. It fell neatly into the hole with a faint clunk. "Great!" cried Trisha.

"Come on," laughed Sam modestly. "You're the one who shot it right next to the hole. It was easy."

"You'd be surprised how many people miss that shot," said Trisha, scooping up the ball. "I can tell, you're a natural at this."

Trisha suggested that they not play a game, but simply practice hitting the ball. That was fine with Sam, and before long she was hitting the ball well. There was something social about golf — it was so different from any other sport she'd ever played. It wasn't fast and thrilling like football or basketball. It was slow and required concentration. Yet, she found it to be unexpectedly exciting. Each time she swung the club she held her breath until the ball stopped moving. Then she immediately began trying to figure how to hit the next shot.

"That was really fun," she told Trisha as they walked off the course. She wiped the perspiration from her forehead. "I can see why people have to get an early start, though. It's too hot out there."

"Would you like to come to the club with me this Friday?" asked Trisha. "I don't work that day. We can get onto that course at dawn if you like."

"What club do you belong to?" asked Sam, trying not to let her excitement show too much.

"The Vista Del Mar. It's pretty stuffy, but Daddy is a member and they have a terrific course." Trisha swept the visor from her head. "It is hot, isn't it," she said, but Sam noticed that she didn't have a drop of perspiration on her. "It's late for the sun to be so blistering."

*Uh-oh*, thought Sam. "What time is it?"

"Just four," said Trisha, checking her delicate gold watch.

"Shoot!" cried Sam. "I was supposed to meet Chris and Liza at four." She handed Trisha her golf club. "Thanks for the lesson. And I would love to come Friday. I'm off then, too. I have to go now."

"Sure, I'll probably see you tomorrow at work," said Trisha with a hint of sulkiness in her voice.

"Okay, thanks again," said Sam. She began to hurry toward the side of the hotel where her bike was chained. Then she stopped and turned back to Trisha. "Thanks again! I had a great time. I wish I didn't have to leave."

Trisha gave her a small quick smile and waved. Hoping she hadn't offended her new friend by dashing off, Sam ran to her bike. She rode home as fast as she could. When she turned up the dirt driveway, Liza and Chris were sitting on the steps of her front porch.

"It's about time," grumbled Liza.

# Chapter Eight

The girls biked through the fancy part of Bonita Beach on the road that led to the best beaches. As she pedaled, Sam kept looking at the mailboxes for the name Royce. She was sure Trisha lived in this part of town, with its high flowering hedges and stately, white two-story houses with sprawling green lawns.

"Let's leave the bikes at Castaway Cove and walk down the shore to the beach," Chris suggested as they rode away from the big houses. "It will look more natural that way, like we were just walking along."

"Good idea," Liza agreed. They stopped at a wooden sign with the name Castaway Cove burned into it. They got off their bikes and walked through a patch of palm trees, along the rocky, narrow path. The cove itself was a sandy little horseshoe-shaped beach, which was very quiet and private. The girls often went there to talk and be alone. The busier beach, the Castaway, was up the shore and around the bend. The water there was rougher and the waves were better for surfing.

The ocean breeze felt good on Sam's slightly sunburned face. The girls leaned their bikes up against the rustling palm trees. Kicking off their sneakers, and leaving the clothing they wore over their suits in a pile on the sand, they scooted down the sandy slope to the sea. In seconds, Sam was off, running and diving into the cool water. Liza was right beside her.

"I'm not getting my hair wet," said Chris, wading in up to her knees. "You know how it looks. Frizz city."

Sam and Liza glanced at one another and laughed. "I think we'd better walk over to see Bruce before she explodes from nervousness," said Liza.

"I think so, too," said Sam, shaking back her long, wet hair.

They got out of the water and headed for the shore. "Wait," said Chris, and ran back for her clothing. She stepped into her shorts and pulled on her oversized pink tie-dyed shirt, leaving it open in front.

"Take that off," said Liza, when Chris caught up with them. "You look fine in the bathing suit. I think you've even lost some weight."

Chris punched her stomach lightly as they

walked along the shore. "I think so, too. It's biking to work every day. Maybe I'll be able to wear a two-piece like you by the end of the summer. Wouldn't that be great?"

"You could wear one now," said Liza. "You're too self-conscious."

"I'm not self-conscious. I'm chubby," said Chris. "When I lose this weight, then I'll reward myself with a two-piece."

Liza tugged at the top of her blue polka-dotted bikini. "I like the way this looks on me, but one-pieces are more comfortable. Which do you like better, Sam?"

"Huh?" Sam asked, roused from her thoughts. "Sorry, I wasn't really listening. I was thinking about golf. Trisha's a great golfer. Do you know she wants to turn pro?"

"That's nice," said Chris, uninterested. They'd rounded the bend in the cove and she'd caught sight of the boys surfing a short distance up the shore. "Do you see Lloyd?" she asked Sam eagerly.

Sam squinted into the sun. "Yeah, I think I see him. I'm sure he's there. When he's not in our kitchen, he's surfing. It's not real hard to track him down."

They walked on until they were right in front of the surfers. "Let's sit down here," Liza suggested.

"Don't you think that's a little obvious?" asked Sam.

"So what?" said Liza. "How else is Lloyd going to see us?"

"There's Bruce, I see him," Chris whispered excitedly. "He's sooo cute!" Sam and Liza looked out to the ocean and saw Bruce bent forward on his yellow board, riding the curl of a wave as it crested behind him.

The girls sat and watched the surfers. In just a few minutes, Lloyd rode a wave in close to shore. He hopped off his board and waded the rest of the way in. He spotted Sam and waved. "Good old Lloyd," said Chris. "Right on cue."

He tucked the board under his arm and joined them on the beach. "Okay, I'm talking to you. Now what?" he asked bluntly.

"Don't slump like that," Sam scolded. "Look like you like us. Laugh or something."

Lloyd threw his head back and soundlessly pretended to be laughing. "You look like a nut, Lloyd," Sam said impatiently.

"Well, what do you want me to do?" Lloyd snapped.

"Just talk to us and act like it's fun," said Sam.

"Be nice, Sam," Chris whispered. "Lloyd is doing me a favor. Thank you, Lloyd."

"I'm glad *somebody* appreciates me," Lloyd said, glaring pointedly at Sam.

"Bruce is getting out of the water," Chris alerted them. "He and his friend are coming this way." She straightened her posture. "Lloyd, it's so good to see you again," she said in a loud voice.

Bruce and his friend walked up to them. "Hi," said Bruce with a wave. "The waves were great today, huh, Lloyd?"

"Super," Lloyd agreed. "Do you know my friends?" he asked Bruce. "My dear, dear friends."

"Sure, I didn't know you guys knew one another though. That's cool," said Bruce. Chris pinched Sam's leg excitedly. The plan was working.

"This is my friend Eddie," Bruce introduced the tall, dark-haired boy beside him.

"Hi," the boy said with a bright smile. "How do you all know the king of the surfers here?"

"Lloyd dates my sister . . . but he and Chris are close friends, have been for years," said Sam.

Lloyd put his arm around Liza. "Yep, Chrissy here is like a sister to me."

"Ha, ha, you're such a joker, Lloyd," said Chris. "You know very well that *I'm* Chris."

"That's me, always joking," said Lloyd, quickly covering his mistake. "You kiddies will have to excuse me, I'm late for supper."

They waved good-bye to Lloyd. "So, you all work at the Palm Pavilion Hotel with Bruce?" asked Eddie.

"We sure do," said Liza, tossing her hair over her shoulder flirtatiously. "Bruce really helped us out today." She went on to tell the story of the ambassador's children and how they'd run off.

". . . and Parker was having a fit, a total fit," she concluded.

"Speaking of fits," said Chris. "A funny thing happened this morning. I was talking about how he would have a fit about something and — "

"And he was right there," Liza jumped in. "But Sam covered it up great . . ." Liza continued to tell the story of how Sam had covered for Chris with Mr. Parker. When she finished talking, there was a lull in the conversation. The five of them stood awkwardly looking at one another.

"That Lloyd is such a tough surfer," Bruce said, breaking the silence. "Where do you know him from, Chris?"

"Chris and I both know him, actually," Liza answered. "He's a doll. So sweet. And I agree, a great surfer."

The conversation went on like that, without any more gaps. Liza took center stage, keeping up a steady chatter. Chris and Sam exchanged knowing glances. It wasn't hard to figure out what was happening. Liza directed almost all her words to Bruce's friend Eddie. With his deep tan and bright blue eyes, he was very good-looking, just the type Liza always liked.

"Want to go for one more ride before we call it quits?" Bruce asked Eddie. Eddie agreed. The two boys said good-bye and ran toward the surf, their boards held over their heads.

"What was that?" Chris demanded angrily the

moment they were out of earshot.

"What was what?" asked Liza innocently.

"You didn't let me say a word!" yelled Chris. "The whole purpose of this was so that I could talk to Bruce."

"You could have cut in," Liza shouted back. "I gave you a chance after I told the story about Sam. You didn't say anything. How come I'm always the one who has to keep up the conversation?"

"How could I say anything?" cried Chris. "Nobody else could say anything with you jabbering away like a parrot."

"Don't get snotty, Chris," said Liza.

"I'm sorry, but I'm mad," Chris insisted. "I was looking forward to this and you hogged the whole show, just because you liked that . . . that guy."

"I did not like him!"

"Oh, come on. You were making googly eyes at him all the while you were talking," said Chris.

"I was not!" yelled Liza.

Sam saw that she was going to have to step in. "Calm down! You *were* kind of flirting with that guy, Liza. But I don't think it matters, Chris. The point is that Bruce saw you with Lloyd, Mr. Surf himself."

"Oh, shut up, Sam," snarled Liza.

"Yeah," Chris agreed. "Mind your own business."

# Chapter Nine

Sam stood at the assignment board checking the day's listing. She caught sight of Liza and Chris hurrying over to her and turned back quickly, pretending not to see them. She was still angry about yesterday afternoon.

"What's the big idea?" Liza asked, coming up beside her.

"Why didn't you wait for us this morning?" Chris asked. "When we got to your house, your mother said you drove in with Greta. How come?"

"I thought we were having a fight," said Sam. "You guys told me to shut up at the beach. We hardly spoke to one another all the way home. I figured you weren't coming by this morning."

"Man!" cried Liza. "How long have the three of us known each other?"

"A long time," Sam answered.

"That's right," Liza agreed. "And don't we *always*

fight over dumb things? And don't we *always* make up the next day?"

"Yeah, but don't you think that's kind of babyish?" Sam objected. "I think fights should have more meaning. What's the purpose of them otherwise?"

Liza and Chris looked at one another. "What do you mean, what's the purpose? There *is* no purpose," said Chris, bewildered. "You get mad, you blow up. Then you cool down and you're friends again."

"Yeah, I admitted to Chris that I was talking too much because I *did* think that Eddie guy was cute," Liza explained. "And when I think a cute boy might like me, I get all nervous."

"And we both know that when Liza is nervous she talks too much," said Chris. "She's been like that since the first grade."

"But I told Chris I would try to be more thoughtful next time and control myself," Liza concluded. "And now the fight is over."

"What about telling me to shut up?" Sam asked in a hurt voice. She wasn't sure she was ready to forget about that. After all, she'd only been trying to help. And she suddenly realized she wasn't only mad about that. She was still angry about the fact that they'd gotten her into trouble for two days running.

"Sam," said Liza, "we'll understand that you can be kind of a know-it-all sometimes, if you forgive us for being so rude to you."

"A know-it-all!" cried Sam. "I am not." How could they say that about her? She simply said what was on her mind.

Liza grinned. "Just a teensy-weensy bit know-it-allish?"

"I guess. Maybe. Sometimes," Sam admitted. Greta was always telling her not to be a such a know-it-all. She supposed there might be a smidgen of truth to it.

"And we were very rude," Chris said apologetically. "There. Now we're all friends again. Right?"

"Right," said Sam with a small smile. It didn't seem worth holding a grudge. Chris and Liza might be a pain sometimes, but they were her best friends.

Liza turned to the bulletin board. "Great," she said, "No Mr. Schwartz again today. Maybe he went home."

"We have the ambassador's kids again, though," Chris noted. "What are we going to do with them today?"

"Take them to the beach like Sam promised," said Liza.

"This morning, when I talked to Mrs. Chan about getting permission to take the kids to the beach, she told me we're going to have them until Saturday," said Sam. "That gave me an idea. Why don't we set up a 'color war' for them and all the other kids who'll be staying until Saturday?"

"What's a 'color war'?" asked Chris.

"Last summer when I went to camp we had one," Sam explained. "You choose sides and name them after colors. Blue team and green team, for instance. Then you play different events and the team that wins the most events wins the prize."

"Sounds good," said Liza, "but what kind of prize would we have?"

"I don't know," Sam said, "maybe Sal at the refreshment bar will donate ice cream sodas or something."

"Good idea!" said Chris. "Let's do it." Then a worried expression suddenly came over her face. "Who wants to be the one to ask Mr. Parker? I don't."

"Me neither," said Sam.

Liza spotted Mr. Parker approaching. "I will," she said bravely. "Oh, yoo-hoo, Mr. Parker," she called to him brightly.

The man stopped, quickly checking Liza's feet to make sure she was wearing the regulation white sneakers. Fortunately, she was. "Yes, Miss Velez," Mr. Parker sighed. "What may I do for you today?"

"Sam has something to ask you," she said.

Sam glared at Liza, but she stepped forward. She quickly explained her idea about the color war. "It would give us a way to get all the kids involved in a project and it might be a lot of fun," she finished.

Mr. Parker looked at the girls thoughtfully. "It sounds fine, but I don't want to say yes right away.

I'm sure there's a potential for disaster here which I have merely failed to identify as of yet."

Chris, Sam and Liza looked at him with puzzled expressions.

"What I mean is that I'm still trying to figure out why this is a bad idea," he explained.

"It's not," said Sam. "I helped run a color war at camp last year. I know how to do it."

"I'll give you an answer tomorrow morning," said Mr. Parker. "I'm sure a good night's sleep will help me uncover the hidden hazards in this venture."

"Tomorrow it will seem like the best idea you've ever heard," said Liza enthusiastically.

Mr. Parker raised an eyebrow. "Yes, no doubt," he said sarcastically. "We will see." With that, he hurried off.

The ambassador's wife appeared in the lobby at that moment. She was wearing a beautiful golden yellow sari. Seven of her children walked behind her, wearing identical white terry beach robes and identical black thongs. Each of them held a neatly folded red beach towel in his or her arms.

"They look like such angels, don't they?" Liza whispered to Chris.

Chris chuckled. "They do while their mother has them."

"I am trusting that you will all behave," the ambassador's wife told her children as Chris, Liza and Sam came to take the kids. The children nodded obediently and their mother left.

"Well, let's go have some fun," said Liza.

"Yaaaahhhhh!" yelled the kids all at once. They tore off through the lobby, charging toward the beach, with Sam, Chris and Liza running behind them. The girls spent an exhausting morning making sand castles, digging holes, throwing beach balls, and explaining that they had no money for ice pops.

Though there was a lifeguard on duty, Sam took charge of the kids in the water. Liza and Chris kept track of them when they were on the land. By two o'clock, the girls had had it. Wearily, they marched their sandy band back to the hotel.

"I hope Parker agrees to the color war," Liza said wearily. "We need some way to use up all the energy these kids have. I can't take another day like today. I'm pooped."

"Me, too," Sam agreed, rubbing the sunburned patch on the back of her neck where she'd forgotten to put tanning lotion.

The ambassador's wife met them in the lobby. She always came and went so quietly it seemed as if she appeared out of thin air. With a polite nod to the girls, she signaled for her children to follow her to the elevator.

As soon as she left, Trisha Royce came up behind Sam. "Are you off?" she asked Sam. Sam nodded. "Want to come to my house for a dip in the pool?"

Sam hesitated. She didn't want to hurt Liza and Chris by not leaving with them two days in a row.

She was eager to see Trisha's house, though.

Liza seized the opportunity to take over. "We'd love to come," she said. "Wouldn't we, Chris?"

"Absolutely," Chris agreed. "We'd love to."

Sam felt her stomach tighten, but she wasn't sure why. Why should it make her tense to spend the afternoon with two old friends and a new one? She didn't know the answer, but something inside told her that this afternoon was going to be bad news.

# Chapter Ten

Liza had never seen a house like Trisha's. It wasn't a mansion, but it wasn't a normal home, either. At least not by Bonita Beach standards. It was white and the middle section had two floors with a two-tiered porch in front. Trisha's house was different because two long one-story extensions had been built onto either side of the house. The one on the left was a giant porch made almost completely of tinted glass.

Liza and Chris walked from the three-car garage, where they'd left their bikes, to the front door. Sam and Trisha had gone ahead with Trisha's father who had come to pick them up. They couldn't see Mr. Royce through the dark, shaded glass of his Cadillac windows.

"Gosh, look at this lawn," said Liza as they walked up the front steps. "I expect to see little flags all over it. It looks like a golf course."

"My Dad would die for this lawn," said Chris.

They climbed the wide porch steps and rang the bell. A maid in a black-and-white uniform answered. "Miss Royce asked that you meet her around back by the pool," the maid said politely.

"Oh, excuse us," Chris said to Liza when the maid had shut the door. "I guess we're not good enough to walk through the house."

"*Miss* Royce, did you hear that?" said Liza. She stuck her finger in her mouth and made a disgusted face. *Yuck!* The girls walked around the side of the glassed-in porch. A hinged opening in the high white fence had been left open for them. As soon as they entered, Liza felt as if she had stepped into another world. A large, oval swimming pool was at the center of the spacious patio. Around it were aqua-blue deck chairs. A matching awning extended out from the house. Sitting under it, drinking from tall glasses, sat Trisha and Sam.

Sam waved her hand to greet them. Chris and Liza waved back and Trisha and Sam got up and walked over to them. Trisha had already changed into a crisp white tennis dress. "We thought we'd play a little tennis," she said.

"What a good idea!" said Liza with false enthusiasm. "I just love tennis." She noticed Chris's puzzled look. Okay, so she wasn't a good tennis player. But she couldn't stand Trisha's superior attitude.

"We have extra rackets in the supply shed by the court," said Trisha. "We can play doubles."

"That would be fine," said Liza. "Just fine."

"I didn't know you could play tennis," said Sam.

Liza tossed back her hair. "There's a lot you don't know about me," she said haughtily.

Sam and Trisha walked slightly ahead of Liza and Chris as they headed across the manicured lawn over to a clay court several yards away. "We don't know how to play tennis," Chris whispered to Liza.

"We had it in gym last year," Liza reminded her. "And remember we went down to the park and practiced."

"And remember we were terrible," added Chris.

"This isn't the Wimbledon tournament. We're only hitting the ball around," Liza pointed out.

"I don't know," said Chris skeptically. "There's something about Trisha that makes me feel very . . . I don't know . . . *fat*."

"Well, she makes me feel too skinny, so don't worry about it," Liza answered. It was true. There was something about Trisha that made Liza feel as if she were talking too loud and that her elbows were bony. Maybe it was her cool grace. Maybe it was her snobbish attitude.

Trisha went into a neat green shed just outside the fenced-in court and came out with four metal rackets and a tall can of tennis balls. "Sam and I will play Christine and Liz," she said.

"Liza," Liza corrected her.

"Sorry," said Trisha.

71

"I think it would be more equal if — " Chris began to object.

"That would be divine," Liza cut her off, taking a racket from Trisha. They stepped out onto the court. Liza and Chris stood on one side of the net, Trisha and Sam on the other.

"You serve first," said Trisha, tossing a bright green ball to Liza.

Liza breathed deeply, trying to remember what she'd learned in gym. She tossed the ball up in the air and swung her racket . . . and the ball rolled across the court.

"Fault!" Trisha called, using the term to indicate the serve was no good.

*Oh, give me a break,* Liza thought as she chased the ball. She brought it back to the baseline and tried again.

"Double fault!" snapped Trisha, as the ball once again rolled away from Liza. "Our serve."

"Try serving it underhand next time," Sam suggested.

Liza smiled at her sourly. "I'm not used to playing with a strange racquet," she said. *And all racquets are strange to me,* she added to herself.

Trisha took the next serve. She slammed the ball cleanly down the middle of the court. Chris and Liza both lunged for it. "Watch out!" Chris cried as she and Liza collided.

"Fifteen, love," Trisha called out the score. She served again. "Thirty, love," she announced as the ball whizzed past Chris. On Trisha's third serve, Liza used two hands and connected with the ball, sending it in a high arc. Sam backed up almost to the fence and lobbed it back. Chris swatted at the returning ball and sent it flying . . . into the net.

"Well, okay!" said Chris. "That was almost a volley."

Trisha didn't seem to share Chris's enthusiasm. "Would you girls mind if Sam and I played a quick game ourselves?" she asked sweetly.

Liza did mind, but she didn't know how to say so. "Sure, go ahead," she said in a sulky tone. She watched as Trisha walked around the net and served to Sam. Sam returned the ball, sailing it about an inch above the net. Trisha returned the ball. They went on without a miss for five full minutes.

"*That* is a volley," Liza whispered to Chris, as they sat on the side and watched.

"I never knew Sam was such a competition freak," Chris commented.

"It's that Trisha. She's so competitive she brings it out in Sam," said Liza.

After the game, Trisha led them all back to the pool. They used an outdoor cabana to change back into the sandy suits they'd worn at the beach that day. Trisha stepped into the house to get her suit. "At least she has a nice pool," said Liza as they waded into the water.

"Are you kidding," quipped Chris. "She has nice everything."

"Except personality," added Liza.

"What's wrong with her personality?" Sam challenged. "She's being nice to you."

"Oh, come on, Sam," said Liza, annoyed. "She's barely tolerating us. She only wants to be friendly with you, not us."

"That's not true," Sam objected. But from the lack of conviction in her voice, Liza knew that Sam knew she was right.

At that moment Trisha emerged from her house wearing a white racing suit and a cap. Two pairs of swimming goggles dangled from her hand. She tossed one to Sam. "Want to race?" she asked.

"Sure," said Sam, putting on the goggles.

In a minute the two girls were off, splashing across the pool. "Ha! Beat you!" Trisha cried happily as she slapped the end of the pool seconds before Sam got there.

"You're terrific!" Sam said, admiration filling her voice.

After their swim, they went up to the sitting area under the awning. "Maria, more lemonades," Trisha told a young woman in a simple pink housecoat.

*What's the magic word?* thought Liza angrily. Trisha's tone of voice irritated her. *Is it so hard to say please or thank you?* Sam didn't seem to notice any of it. She appeared to be totally enthralled with Trisha.

Liza sat back and watched as Sam hung on every word the girl said. She knew that Sam admired heroes. She remembered the time back in third grade when Sam plastered her wall with pictures of famous women athletes. The skater Dorothy Hamill had been her favorite. Sam had devoted one wall to her alone. It hadn't bothered Liza then. That was how Sam was. She looked up to people who were good at sports.

But this was different. It seemed to Liza that Sam was looking to model herself after this girl—and it wasn't only because she was good in sports. Liza could see Sam taking on her manner of speaking. She even detected in Sam an imitation of Trisha's fluid, hips-forward walk.

And it was bugging Liza to death! She didn't want to lose her friend. And she certainly didn't want to see her turn into a phony like Trisha Royce. . . .

"You want to be a lifeguard, too!" Sam exclaimed, interrupting Liza's thoughts.

Trisha got up from the table. "I'll bring out some of my racing medals," she said, heading into the house.

"I can't believe this!" said Sam. "We have so much in common."

Liza turned to Chris and placed her hand on her shoulder. "We have *sooo* much in common," she mimicked bitingly.

75

# Chapter Eleven

Sam wondered if she was imagining things. She had sensed a certain coolness from Chris and Liza ever since their day at Trisha's house. When they came by the next morning to ride to work with her, they were quiet most of the way. And every time Sam mentioned Trisha, they changed the subject.

She wanted to believe Chris and Liza were acting strange, but she had a good idea of how they felt. Trisha just didn't seem to like them. And though she was polite about it, it was hard for her to hide her feelings. Sam didn't blame her. In fact, Sam was suddenly seeing her two best friends through Trisha's eyes. They did seem sort of childish and silly. They just wanted to fool around all the time.

Now she stood at the assignment board in the hotel lobby waiting for them. They'd gone upstairs to the open balcony of the Parrot Lounge to see

Pitpat, their favorite parrot. That was just the kind of thing that bothered her. Chris and Liza knew they weren't allowed up there! Raoul the bartender didn't seem to care, but Mr. Parker would have one of his famous fits if he caught them.

At that moment, she saw Mr. Parker approaching. "Miss O'Neill," he called, in his serious voice. He stood beside her tapping his pen on his clipboard. It seemed to Sam that even when Mr. Parker was standing still, he was moving. "I have considered your request for a competition and have failed to come up with any objections. Though I'm sure I shall rue the day I consented, you have my permission to proceed."

"That's great, Mr. Parker," said Sam. "You won't regret it."

"I have one requirement," he said. "You and your cronies, Misses Brown and Velez, are the only sitters I can spare to help. I need the other baby sitters to care for any children not wishing to participate."

Sam considered that. "I think we really need two co-captains on each team," she said. Then she had an idea. "If Trisha from the Pro Shop can arrange her schedule, do you think she could help out?"

"You know Trisha?" Mr. Parker asked, arching one eyebrow in surprise. Sam didn't like his tone. It was as if he were saying, *I can't believe a known criminal like you knows such a well-bred young lady.*

"Yes, I played tennis with her yesterday," Sam

77

heard herself say in a false voice that she barely recognized.

"If Trisha is willing to join you in this escapade, I don't have any objections. In fact, I would feel relieved to know there was a level-headed influence being introduced into the situation."

Ordinarily Sam would have been annoyed by Mr. Parker's last remark. After all, he was not exactly voicing his faith in her, but right now, she didn't care. The important thing was that he'd said yes to the competition. It would be lots of fun for the kids and even more fun now that Trisha could be involved.

"I'll ask her right now," Sam told Mr. Parker. "She's right over there," she added, pointing across the lobby at Trisha, who was about to go into the Pro Shop.

"Very good," said Mr. Parker. He turned to leave and then turned back. "By the way, where are your two notorious associates this fine morning?"

Sam looked at him, not quite understanding.

"Where are Miss Velez and Miss Brown?" he clarified his meaning. "You look somehow incomplete standing there without them."

"Oh, they're here," Sam said, being intentionally vague. "You know how they always have to be doing something. They're probably helping Mrs. Chan with — "

Just then there was a loud screeching from the Parrot Lounge. Sam and Mr. Parker both looked up to see Liza at the railing, hanging on to one of Pitpat's legs, as the bird tried to make its escape. Chris was beside her, hopping up and down anxiously.

Liza noticed Mr. Parker right away. "No problem!" she called down as she struggled with the bird, his wings flapping furiously. "I've got him."

"Everything's under control!" Chris yelled down over the railing.

Sam and Mr. Parker watched as Liza got a better grip on the bird and tucked him under one arm. They disappeared into the back of the lounge, where the bird's perch stood.

Mr. Parker looked at Sam and then back up at the Parrot Lounge. He rubbed his forehead and seemed to decide against exploding. "Yes, everything is under control," he muttered to himself. "Everything is under control. That will be my thought for the day." He walked off, still muttering, "Everything is under control. Everything is under control."

"Nice going," said Sam when Chris and Liza joined her at the board.

"It wasn't our fault," said Chris. "Whoever fastened the lock to Pitpat's cord didn't close it right. His foot slipped right through."

"I think it was Chef Alleyne. He's always saying how Pitpat is a noble creature and needs to be free," added Liza. "I think I deserve thanks for catching him."

"You're not even supposed to be up there," Sam reminded them. "But listen, Mr. Parker said we can run our competition."

"Great!" said Liza. "What do we do first?"

"Well, I'm going to ask Trisha if she can be my co-captain. Parker said he could only spare the three of us and we need a fourth person."

"Why her?" asked Liza indignantly.

"She's good at sports and she's a friend of ours," Sam defended her choice.

"A friend of *yours*, you mean," said Chris.

"Okay, she's my friend. And I think she'd be good. I have to go ask her first, anyway."

"Well, don't let us stop you," Liza snapped. "Just don't take too long. We have the ambassador's kids again today. Chris and I don't want to be stuck with them by ourselves while you two discuss your tennis right hand."

"Backhand," Sam corrected her.

"Whatever," Chris said impatiently.

"Don't be such crabs," said Sam. "This is going to be fun." She headed across the lobby to the Pro Shop. Trisha was already behind the counter when Sam came through the door.

"Hi," she said, smiling.

"Hi," Sam returned the greeting. Every time she saw Trisha she was struck by how put-together she looked. Today her smooth blond hair was held back by a thin blue silk band. Even though she wore the hotel polo shirt, hers somehow looked neater and newer than anyone else's. Even her light golden tan was perfect — not uneven and peeled like Sam's skin always looked by the end of the summer.

She told Trisha about the hotel competition and asked if she would be a co-captain with her. "That works out wonderfully," said Trisha. "The shop is going to be painted and re-carpeted in the next three days. I'm completely free. It sounds fantastic."

"I'm so glad you're going to be part of this," said Sam.

"Oh, so am I," said Trisha. "Who will be on the other team?"

"Chris and Liza."

"Oh," said Trisha dryly.

Sam opened her mouth to defend her friends. She was going to urge Trisha to give Liza and Chris a chance. But she decided to say nothing. They hadn't given Trisha a chance. Besides, Sam was tired of being the peacemaker.

"You'll be working with me, not them," Sam informed Trisha.

Trisha's face brightened. "Okay, I'll do it!"

"Great, it'll be fun," said Sam.

"Fun, nothing!" said Trisha enthusiastically. "This is a competition, isn't it? This means war!"

# Chapter Twelve

Sam got paper and pens from Mrs. Chan and set to work on announcements about the hotel competition. "The Palm Pavilion's Very First Sports Spectacular!" she wrote in bright red. "To be held this Saturday. All children over the age of five are invited to join. Sign up at one o'clock today at the snack bar. Compete for fun and prizes!"

She looked at her sign and then added a squiggly drawing of some kids throwing a ball. "There," she said, pleased with her sign. She posted it on the announcement board in the lobby and then made four more and tacked them up near the elevators where they couldn't be missed.

"Are you done?" Chris asked, when Sam returned from the last elevator. "These kids are getting restless." She and Liza had the kids in the lobby waiting for Sam so they could go outside. Seven-year-old Ismail took hold of Sam's hand as they walked to the pool.

"Ismail is a baby," Dira taunted her brother.

The boy just stuck his tongue out at his sister and kept hold of Sam's hand. "I like you," he said to Sam.

"I like you, too," Sam answered. As they walked, she thought about how much she really did like Ismail — and most of the kids she babysat. They were so innocent and funny. She decided to spend the day just thinking about the kids and not worrying about anything else.

They spent the morning in the pool. The girls led them in a game of volleyball using a big inflatable ball at the shallow end of the pool. "This sports idea is good," Chris admitted as she tossed the ball back into play. "Giving them a special activity uses up their energy, and they're not running all over the place."

Sam nodded. She reached high to catch the ball as it was almost tossed out of the pool. Ismail had hit it up and back over his head. "Not such a good hit," said his sister Rekha.

"Ismail is a bad sport!" cried Kashi.

"He's not a bad sport," said Sam. "He's a good sport. He just didn't hit the ball right that time." Liza caught the ball and threw it back to the boy. "Try again," Sam said.

Ismail tried to serve the ball, and this time it flew sideways into the deeper water. Ismail looked at Sam, his big brown eyes wide with apology.

83

"Kashi is right. I am a bad sport."

"No, no," Sam explained as she waded out to retrieve the floating ball. "You're a good sport because you don't get angry when you lose. A bad sport throws tantrums, and doesn't accept defeat gracefully."

"Ismail is always defeated," Naima offered.

"He isn't defeated. He tries and that's what counts. Maybe sports isn't his thing. I'm sure he does other things well," Sam said as she carried the ball back.

"Ismail draw birds. Pretty birds," shouted little Nahib.

"Yes, Ismail is the best artist of us all," Rekha said.

"There you go," Liza said, catching the ball Sam tossed to her. "Everybody does something well."

The game lasted until lunch. Then they marched the kids up to Sal's refreshment bar and billed the food to Ambassador Rama's room. Soon it was one o'clock and kids began coming to the snack bar from all directions.

"Hi, there," said Trisha, coming up behind two little girls who were signing up for the competition. "They closed the Pro Shop at noon for painting, so I'm all yours."

"Lucky us," Chris whispered to Liza.

By ten after one, there were at least fifteen kids assembled. "Okay," Sam told them. "I'm Sam. This is Trisha. We're going to head up the Green Team.

Over there are Chris and Liza. They're captains of the Blue Team."

"We don't even get to pick our own color?" Liza objected.

Sam sighed impatiently. "What color would you like?"

Liza looked at Chris who shrugged her shoulders. She thought a moment. "Blue is nice," she conceded.

Sam rolled her eyes and continued. "Now we're going to choose up sides. When you've been picked, tell me your name and team and I'll write it down."

"I pick you . . . and you," Trisha began sorting through the kids. "You're on the Green Team . . . and you."

"Get in there," Chris urged Liza. "She's picking all the best kids."

"Me? What about you?" said Liza. "I can't tell which kids would be good."

Chris got up and looked at the kids, but she saw that she was too late. Every kid who looked athletic was already taken. She was left with the skinny, the fat, and the shy-looking ones.

"Hey, can I still sign up?" asked a red-haired boy with stocky arms and broad shoulders. He was running toward the snack bar eagerly.

"He's ours!" Chris cried, putting her hand on the boy's shoulders.

Ismail raised his hand. "I would like to be on the

team with Miss Sam, since she is my friend," he requested.

Trisha looked at Sam and shook her head no. Sam understood why. Ismail certainly wouldn't be an asset to the team. But how could she say no? "Come on," she said to Ismail, pretending she hadn't noticed Trisha.

"All right," Liza announced. "All of you be right here tomorrow at nine-thirty for practice." All the kids dispersed except for the Rama children.

"Let's go back to the lobby," said Chris. "It's time for their mother to pick them up." As they walked the children back, Sam told the other three of her plans for the different events. She thought they should have a volleyball game like the one they'd played today, as well as a relay race, a sack race, and a diving board competition.

"These kids can't dive," Liza objected.

"They don't have to," Sam explained. "They can do funny stuff like cannonballs and leaps and backward drops."

"We need slogans," said Trisha. "I know—Go Green machine!"

"Yeah!" cried Sam, getting swept up into the spirit. "Go for the gold with Green!"

"Green is great!" cried Trisha.

Sam looked to Liza and Chris for their slogans. "I don't know," Chris admitted.

Liza shrugged. "Blue is beautiful? No, maybe not. I'll have to think about it."

"That's terrible," said Sam.

"We're not into slogans, okay?" Chris said irritably.

Sam was glad she had a spirited partner like Trisha. What fun was a competition if you didn't at least try to win?

# Chapter Thirteen

Sam tried not to be so excited as she walked up the path to Trisha's house, her sister Greta's overnight bag in her hand. It was the Friday before the big competition and Trisha had invited her to stay over. She said they needed to work on their team strategy.

Greta and Lloyd had dropped her off. She was ashamed of herself, but she wished Greta would hurry and pull her clunker of a car out of the driveway before anyone answered the door. It looked so out of place standing in front of the elegant house. She looked back and waved to Greta, as if to say everything was fine, she could go. But the car stood in the drive, its muffler announcing that it needed repair loud enough for the whole neighborhood to hear.

The door opened and a balding man of about fifty dressed in a gray business suit appeared.

"Mr. Royce?" Sam guessed. "I'm here to see Trisha."

Seeing that someone had answered the door, Greta honked and pulled out of the driveway, her muffler rumbling even more loudly. A look of concern came over Mr. Royce's face and he stepped out onto the porch to see what was causing the noise.

"That's just my sister. She dropped me off," Sam explained, mortified.

Mr. Royce studied her for a second and then smiled the same quick smile as Trisha. "Come right in. I didn't catch your name."

"Samantha O'Neill," Sam said, somehow thinking he would like her better with a more formal name.

Up until that moment, she hadn't been inside Trisha's spectacular home. She had imagined it would be nice, but she wasn't quite prepared for what she saw. The living room to her right was filled with sofas and straight-back chairs all upholstered in the same rich, silky flowered material. Thick, white carpeting ran through the living room into a lavish dining area to her left. The large, dark mahogany table was polished to a high gleam.

It seemed to Sam that her whole house could fit into these two rooms. And she knew that white carpet wouldn't stay white for long — not with Trevor running around, and the parts from her father's boat motor piled in the corner. She definitely could not picture five bowls of Chompy Pet dog food laid out across this floor!

"Hi, there," said Trisha, coming down the stairs. "I see you've met Daddy." Her father nodded sternly, clearly uninterested in further conversation. He walked down the hall.

"Don't mind him," Trisha whispered. "It's Mario's night off and he hates having to answer the door."

Sam stifled a smile. Somehow she couldn't picture her father being annoyed about answering the door. It was one of those things people just did. The idea of a stranger living in your house whose job it was to open the door seemed absurd.

"Let's go upstairs," said Trisha, grabbing Sam's scruffy bag.

Sam followed her up to her room. "Wow!" she exclaimed, despite her efforts to be cool. Trisha had a double bed all to herself. It was covered with a white eyelet bedspread. Beautiful pillows in different colors were piled high on the bed. "How do you get this bed together every morning?" Sam asked. "I'm lucky if mine even gets made."

Trisha laughed. "Linda, the day maid, takes care of all that. I certainly wouldn't make it. I don't even know how to make a bed."

"It's easy," said Sam. "All you do is — "

"Forget it," Trisha stopped her. "I don't want to know. Why learn something I'll probably never have to do?"

"I guess," agreed Sam. It was mind-boggling to

imagine a life in which you might never have to make a bed. It sounded nice, though.

"We have got to win that competition tomorrow," Trisha said, lying across the white bed.

"I don't think we have to worry," Sam said as she settled down on a cushiony white armchair in the corner of the room. "We have all the best kids."

"Not exactly," Trisha reminded her. "We got stuck with that Ismail kid who likes you so much."

Sam laughed lightly. "He's not much of an athlete, but he is a cute kid."

"We have to find a way to keep him from competing," said Trisha seriously. "We could keep moving him to the back of the line. Or maybe we can put him in charge of something dumb. Call him royal towel holder, or something."

"He's pretty bright," objected Sam. "He'd figure out what we were doing."

Trisha sighed. "I wish we hadn't gotten stuck with him. Did you see him at practice today? He can't do anything."

"He *is* a klutz." Sam laughed. "But he'll be all right."

"I hope so. I really want to win this thing." Trisha got up from the bed and opened her large closet door. "Want to borrow one of my dresses? Daddy likes people to dress for dinner."

"Sure," said Sam. She walked to the closet and looked through the two levels of clothing. She didn't care much for dresses, but these were nice

91

ones, sporty and tailored. She picked out a plain white shift in a heavy cotton. "Think this would fit?" she asked.

"That'll look great on you," Trisha answered.

Sam stepped out of her shorts and T-shirt and pulled the dress on over her head. "Winning this thing is important to you, isn't it," Sam noted as she wiggled into the square-cut armholes of the dress.

"Of course," said Trisha, stepping into a white cotton skirt. "My father is a trial lawyer. He says he's so successful because he won't accept any other outcome but to win his case. If you want to be an athlete you have to think that way, too."

Sam strained to button up the back of her dress. Trisha came behind and helped her. "Is it important to always win, though?" Sam asked.

"My father says it's a way of life. Either you're a winner or a loser. If you're a winner, then that's what you always try to do. You win. Doesn't that make sense to you?"

"I'm not sure," Sam answered honestly. "It sounds like it makes sense . . . but I don't know."

Trisha stood in front of her full-length wall mirror and began brushing her silky hair. "It does make sense. The problem is that there are more losers than winners in this world. Take your two friends for example. They are *not* winners."

"Maybe not the way you mean," said Sam, "but — "

92

"Not in any way. They just don't care."

"But that doesn't make them losers," Sam protested.

"Are they going to lose tomorrow?" Trisha asked, stepping into a pair of white sandals.

Sam shrugged. "I'm pretty sure."

"Then they're losers. Frankly, Sam, I don't know why you hang out with them. They make you look bad. You're a winner, but they aren't."

Sam didn't know what to say. She knew that Liza and Chris didn't fit into Trisha's definition of winners. But to call them losers? That seemed awfully harsh.

They went downstairs and seated themselves at the long table. Sam thought that she'd finally get to meet Trisha's mother, but no one appeared except Mr. Royce. The same woman who had brought the lemonade the other day served dinner. The thick steak and mashed potatoes were delicious, but Mr. Royce barely spoke and the dinner was eaten mostly in silence. Sam couldn't get used to it; it was so different from her house, where supper was a noisy, dish-clattering event full of lively chatter.

After dinner the girls went back to Trisha's room and discussed the competition. They went over their strategies, and talked about which kids should start and which should finish in each event.

Later, they watched a movie on the VCR in

Trisha's room. It was a silly comedy about college students during spring break.

"Trisha?" Sam asked, as the light from the TV played across their faces. "Where is your mother?"

Trisha continued to stare at the TV. "She left when I was small. I don't really remember much about her. But my father says she was definitely a loser."

Sam suddenly felt very uncomfortable and pretended to be watching the TV intently. *Poor Trisha!* she thought. *It would be so sad not to have your mother around — even if she was a loser.* She wondered what Mrs. Royce had been like. What made someone a loser according to Trisha and her father? Would they think *her* mother was a loser?

Sam tried to shake the unpleasant thoughts from her head. She didn't want to dwell on them. All she knew was that she was glad her mother was at home — loser or not.

# Chapter Fourteen

"That's it. These posters must come down," Mr. Parker insisted, ripping one off a wall. "This is not the image we are trying to create at the Palm Pavilion."

Sam had to admit they had gotten carried away. She and Trisha were most at fault, too. They had placed Green Team posters just about everywhere. "Don't worry," Sam assured him, pulling another poster off a column. "We don't need them anymore. The event is today, in an hour."

"Make sure they come down," he repeated. At that moment, the sound of young voices singing made Mr. Parker turn.

Over in one corner of the lobby, Liza and Chris had assembled their team and were leading them in a rousing song. "We will win, that is true. We will win, 'cause we're true blue! Green is glum, they're on the run. We'll beat them, through and through. We're the best, 'cause we're true blue!" Chris and Liza were both wearing blue shorts and matching blue bows in their hair. Sam noticed that Liza had even sprayed a blue streak onto her long hair.

Sam saw the members of her team coming together near the front desk. She gathered them around her and led a cheer. "Green is keen, here's what we mean. Green, green, the greatest team you've ever seen!" She made up the chant on the spot. She repeated it and the kids picked it right up.

She looked the kids over and noticed that Ismail was missing. "Where is your brother?" Sam asked Naima.

"He did not want to disgrace his team," the little girl told her. "He says he will not come out of the room until after the games."

Mr. Parker walked up to Sam. "Take this awful cacophony of youthful exuberance outside, if you please," he said to Sam as the Blue Team tried to drown out the Green's chant.

Trisha walked up to the group at that moment. "Okay, team, let's go outside," she said, smiling confidently at Mr. Parker. She'd come appropriately dressed, of course, with a green headband and kelly green shorts. "Ready to win?" she asked Sam.

"Sure am," Sam answered. "Take the kids over by the pool. I'll be right back."

"Everything all right?" Trisha asked.

"Yeah, I'll be right there," Sam answered. She walked down the hall and took the express elevator to the seventeenth floor. She was greeted by the same man with the walkie-talkie she'd encountered last week.

"Now what?" he asked, when the elevator door opened.

"I'm Ismail Rama's baby sitter and Green Team captain," she said, trying to sound extra-official. "I wish to see the ambassador's son."

"Wait here," said the man, disappearing into the ambassador's suite. He returned and, without saying another word, held the door open for her.

She stepped into the large suite with its pale green furnishings and plate glass windows overlooking the ocean. Immediately she spotted Ismail sitting at the elevated dining area, hunched over the table, his head in his hands. "Come on, you're going to be late," she said.

Mrs. Rama emerged from the bedroom. "Ismail feels it would be best if he did not join in," she said. "He is a sensitive boy. I do not want to force him."

"Oh, no, we need him," said Sam, more to Ismail than to Mrs. Rama.

Ismail glanced up at her. "Do you really need me?" he asked with a small smile.

"Of course!" Sam insisted. "We're a team and the team needs all its members."

"You want me on your team?"

97

"I'm counting on you," Sam said heartily. "Come on, get ready."

Smiling broadly, Ismail grabbed his towel off the chair. "I have already my bathing suit on," he announced happily. Then his face turned serious. "I might not be so good."

"You'll be fine," Sam said, putting her hand on his narrow shoulder.

"Good luck," said his mother, blowing him a kiss at the door.

When Sam and Ismail got down to the pool area, the kids were already assembled on the beach. The first event was to be the sack race.

Liza and Chris had their team ready. "Look out! We're starting off with our ace-in-the-hole, our human dynamo, Bobby!" said Chris, pointing to the stocky, red-haired boy who had signed up for the competition at the last minute.

Trisha handed Naima Rama her burlap bag. "He'll have to be fast to beat Naima here!" she called back.

A small group of parents had assembled to watch the event. Sam was chagrined to see that Mr. Parker was among the spectators. Now they *really* couldn't afford to have anything go wrong.

She looked into the crowd and saw that Bruce Johnson and his friend Eddie were also there. Bruce wasn't wearing the hotel uniform, so this must be his day off. She wanted to go over to Chris and tell her how great that was, but it suddenly didn't feel right. She realized she was no longer confident about where her friendship with Liza and Chris stood. Up until that moment it hadn't hit her just how far apart they'd drifted. But this morning there was no denying it. They hadn't come by to get her and they hadn't spoken to her once all morning. She felt as if there was a great emptiness in the pit of her stomach all of a sudden.

"Where did he come from?" Trisha came over and whispered.

"Who?" Sam asked.

"That little klutzy kid. For a minute I thought we'd gotten lucky and he wasn't coming," said Trisha, gesturing toward Ismail.

"He'll be okay," said Sam.

"I hope so," Trisha said doubtfully.

The kids were assembled for the sack race in two lines. The first in each line — Naima on the Green Team, Bobby on the Blue — stepped into long burlap bags which had been used to hold potatoes. Sam had gotten them from the hotel's kitchen. The object of the race was to hop to your team captain at the finish line, slap her hand, and hop back. Then the bag was passed to the next person in line, who had to do the same thing.

The Green Team won the sack race, but it was a closer competition than Sam had expected. Bobby was indeed a human dynamo, agile and fast. He gave his team a strong lead. And the Green Team lost a lot of time when Ismail tumbled in the sand. He squirmed in his bag and had difficulty righting himself. Still, the Green Team was able to catch up and win.

"You see? I am not so good," he said to Sam after the race.

"We won, didn't we?" Sam cheered him up. "The whole team won, and you're on the team."

The game of water volleyball was equally close. Again, even though his teammates were fairly useless, Bobby managed to act like a one-kid ball return service. To everyone's surprise, the Blue Team won that event.

The next two events had the teams neck and neck — the Blues won the relay and the Greens took the crabwalking contest.

"I can't believe it's a tie score," Trisha said.

"I know," laughed Sam incredulously. "It's that Bobby kid. He's unbelievable."

"And we have that Ismail kid. He's unbelievable, too — unbelievably bad. Can't we donate him to the Blue Team or something?"

"Trisha!" Sam gasped.

"Just kidding," said Trisha, but Sam wasn't so sure that she really was.

It was time for the board-jumping event. This would be the tie-breaker. The largest pool of the three had two diving boards that stood side by side. The rule was that each kid had to walk to the end of the board and do a cannonball or some kind of funny jump into the water and then swim to the side. Only kids who had proved they could swim and jump from the board during practice were allowed to participate.

"Blue is the color of water!" Liza cheered. "We're going to win it!"

"True Blue! True Blue!" Chris led her team in a chant.

Trisha started a counter cheer. "Green is great! Green is great!" she shouted.

The lifeguard on duty blew her whistle. "Remember, no running, and no one jumps until the person ahead is out of the water," she reminded them. "The first team that finishes wins."

The event got off to a bad start for the Greens when a little girl named Patty couldn't find her noseplugs. She got into an argument with her sister Kerry about who actually owned the noseplugs Kerry was wearing around her neck.

Kerry and Patty had been at the front of the line. By the time Trisha moved them to the back, the Blue Team had a solid lead. It seemed that jumping off a diving board was something they all did with little fear.

"We're going to lose!" Trisha whispered to Sam, a panicked edge to her voice. "And look who's up next."

Sam watched as Ismail hesitated at the back of the board. Yesterday in practice he had been a little nervous on the board. Sam had gotten into the water with her arms outstretched as Ismail sat on the end of the board and let himself fall forward.

"That was good!" she'd told him as he came to the surface, smiling.

"I will do better tomorrow," he had assured her.

Now he was moving slowly out onto the middle of the board. Sam could see he was scared. His skinny knees were almost visibly quivering. He looked all around, obviously intimidated by all the spectators.

"Okay, Ismail. Thatta boy!" Sam cheered him on.

While Ismail made his hesitant approach, the Blue Team to the side was busy flinging themselves off the board with abandon.

"True blue! True blue!" the kids cheered, thrilled to have victory so close.

"Move!" Sam heard Trisha shriek at the boy. "Move, for heaven's sake!"

lsmail looked at her and folded his arms across his chest nervously. He walked out to the end of the board and stopped. "Move!" Trisha screamed again.

Sam saw tears coming to the boy's eyes. He wasn't moving. He was standing there, terrified. Sam could tell that he a had a terrible case of nerves. "Come back, Ismail!" she called.

Ismail didn't move. Sam could see he was panicking. "Can you come back?" she called to him. He shook his head. "Can you jump?" she asked. Again, he shook his head no.

Realizing that he was frozen with fear, Sam

kicked off her sneakers, climbed the short ladder, and stepped out onto the board. She put her arms around his shoulder. "Okay, sweetie, it's okay. Come on back with me. I'm here," she said.

Ismail began to move back, but then he stopped. He seemed to spot something at the side of the pool. Sam followed his gaze. The first thing she saw was the security man with the walkie-talkie, still wearing his blue suit. Then she noticed Mr. Parker, and beside him she saw Ambassador Rama. It was easy to pick him out with his long, flowing white jacket, and white baggy pants.

She saw Ismail inhale deeply at the sight of his father. Then with a wild yell, and his arms and legs flying, Ismail threw himself into the pool.

# Chapter Fifteen

"You're fired!" Mr. Parker exploded, bending down so that he was practically nose to nose with Sam.

"But . . . but . . . why?" Sam stammered.

"Ambassador Rama saw you push his son off the board. Was it that important to win this little contest?"

"But I didn't push him," Sam protested. "He jumped." Sam turned to Trisha for support. "You saw him jump, didn't you?"

"I really didn't see what happened," she said. "I told you not to go up on that board, though."

Sam's jaw dropped. "You did not!"

"Sam, please, I have to tell the truth," Trisha said innocently.

Sam looked for Ismail, but he had been upset by all the commotion and seemed to be ashamed of having gotten Sam into trouble. He had walked off holding his mother's hand. Tears of anger and humiliation filled Sam's eyes. She didn't want anyone to see her cry. She grabbed up her shorts and sneakers and rushed away.

"Sam!" Liza cried as Sam ran past with her head bent.

"Just leave me alone!" she shouted at Liza. She had to get out of there. How had everything gone so terribly wrong?

She ran straight up to the bike rack and unchained her bike. She saw Chris's and Liza's bikes a few rungs over, standing chained together. She jumped on her bike and rode away from the hotel as fast as she could, tears blinding her as she pedaled.

When she got to her house, she stopped at the beginning of the drive. She sniffed and wiped away her tears. She didn't want anyone to ask her what had happened. She was too embarrassed. To be fired! She — the sensible one. And why had Trisha betrayed her like that?

Boy! Had she ever been wrong about Trisha! She'd thought Trisha was so cool — nothing seemed to rattle her. But Trisha had deserted her as soon as Mr. Parker barked. Not only deserted her, but turned on her! *I told you not to go on that board!* Trisha's words of betrayal rang in Sam's ears. That was an out-and-out lie. Trisha hadn't said anything like that.

Sam had never experienced this kind of awful feeling. It was as if there were a terrible emptiness inside her. She had idolized Trisha, wanted to be just like her. She was so disappointed — and so hurt.

Up the drive, her father was loading his van with supplies for his afternoon snorkeling trip. He always did a morning and afternoon trip and came home for lunch in between. He spotted her standing in the drive and waved. *Rats! Now I can't sneak in,* Sam realized. She got off her bike and walked it up to the house.

She was almost at the porch when Trevor burst through the screen door, a large bag of Chompy Pet dog food over his head. He was in a panic, barking and waving his head, unable to get the bag off.

Mrs. O'Neill was close on his heels. She danced around him, trying to remove the bag. Finally she got hold of a corner and managed to pull it off. Small, brown morsels of Chompy Pet stuck to Trevor's fur. The little bit that was left in the half-empty bag poured out onto the floor. Mrs. O'Neill looked at the bag. "Hey, it's the Seafood Delight. He likes it."

Mr. O'Neill let out a loud belly laugh. Mrs. O'Neill laughed, too. Sam joined them, but somewhere, mid-laugh, something inside her turned and before she knew it, she had burst into tears.

Her parents stopped laughing. "What's wrong?" her mother asked, hurrying down the porch steps.

"I got fired!" Sam blurted out. Her father handed her his blue bandana and she dried her eyes. She

106

told them the whole story. " . . . and Trisha knew I didn't push him, but she didn't stick up for me," she concluded.

"What about Liza and Chris?" her mother asked.

"They were watching their own kids," she explained with a sniffle, "and besides, I think they're mad at me anyway."

"I see," said her mother. "It sounds very unfair."

"Darned unfair," her father agreed.

"You must be so disappointed in me," said Sam. "I mean, I got fired. Fired!" She still couldn't believe it.

"Sam," said her father calmly. "We would be disappointed in you only if you did something wrong. Being fired is nothing to be embarrassed about. Some bosses are impossible to work for."

"That's Mr. Parker," Sam said sullenly. "He didn't even give me a chance to explain."

"See what I mean," said her father.

"But I love babysitting," said Sam, starting to feel weepy again. "And it was my very first real job."

Her father put his arm around her shoulder. "You're not out of work," he said. "I need a first mate today. Al felt sick after this morning's tour. I was going to do the afternoon run without him, but I could sure use your help."

"I don't know," said Sam. "I feel kind of crummy."

"No sense sitting around brooding about it," her mother advised. "Go with Daddy."

107

"Maybe you're right," Sam agreed. Her father handed her a coil of rope.

"Throw this in the back of the van and we'll be off," he said, opening the driver's door of the van.

Sam threw in the rope and hopped into the van beside her father. They were soon rattling down the dirt road that led to the small cabin and inlet where her father kept his boat. A sign on the road said: This Way to Captain Dan's World Famous Snorkeling Tours. Greta had painted it in the same flowery script as the sign on the van.

They pulled into the dirt lot, where a group of people were already waiting. Mr. O'Neill adjusted his captain's hat and stepped out. He greeted the people with a jolly, almost theatrical manner that always embarrassed Sam. "Hello there, every-body!" he boomed. "Ready to look at some fishies? Come to think of it, some of you look a little fishy to me, yourselves. But what the heck! I'm sure you're fine folks, and the fish are awaiting your arrival. So, let's get going."

A man named Paul who worked with her father stepped out of the small cabin. He'd been taking payment from the people and handing out snorkeling equipment. "Hi, there, kiddo," he greeted her with his lively Jamaican lilt. "You've grown some long legs since I last saw you."

"I guess," Sam said.

"You going to help us today?"

Sam nodded. "Good thing. Glad to see you," he

said. He moved to the rear of the medium-sized cabin cruiser and called out, "Step this way! Captain Dan's boat is about to embark on another exciting cruise."

Sam hadn't been on one of these cruises in about a year. She'd almost forgotten what a show Paul and her father put on for people. Her father had once told her that it made the event more fun for everyone. From the smiles on everyone's faces, she could see that it worked.

The group of fourteen people got onto the boat. There were three ladies with white hair who seemed to be together and four couples in their twenties. There was also a short, bald man with his two teenaged sons. Sam couldn't help noticing that one of them, a nice-looking boy with longish blond hair, was noticing her, too.

Sam helped Paul untie the boat from its mooring and then she hopped in. Her father was soon maneuvering the craft through shallower waters, past high, grassy patches of land and large rocks. When they hit the open water, he revved the engine full throttle and they sped out to sea.

Sam realized that her father had been right. The wind in her face and the salt air made her feel much better. She climbed to the front of the boat and sat by herself, turning her face up to the sun. The boat eventually stopped, seemingly in the middle of nowhere. "Below us are some of the finest coral reefs you will ever see," her father announced to his guests. "And where there is coral, there are all kinds of ocean creatures. You won't have to look hard to find them."

Sam climbed down from the front of the boat. Mr. O'Neill lifted up her arm. "This is my daughter, Samantha. I taught her to snorkel before she could walk, so she will be happy to assist you in any way. Paul over there is an honorary fish, so he, too, can help you with whatever you need. They will be in the water with you. I will be up here. Happy snorkeling."

Sam showed the white-haired ladies how to rub their masks with saliva to keep them from fogging underwater, and how to attach their air pipes.

When everyone was in their gear, they jumped overboard. "Make sure nobody gets stuck to a rock or attacked by a barracuda or anything," said her father as Sam prepared to go over.

"Okay," she said, smiling at him. Sam plunged down into the silent underwater world. Immediately a yellow-striped angelfish swam past her goggles. She swam to the surface, blew the water from her air tube and then continued to swim with the top of the tube above the surface. The water was relatively shallow here and it was easy to see the bottom.

When Sam snorkeled she always imagined she was flying over some strange, exotic planet. The coral — some pink, some white, some yellowish brown — attracted many kinds of fish to it. She saw an iridescent parrot fish with its blue, green and orange stripes swim by. A small school of purple fish Sam couldn't name hovered, feeding off the coral. Below them, a rock lobster slowly made its way along the sandy bottom.

A wonderful calm came over Sam. The fish barely paid attention to her. They were living their lives in this colorful world, not worrying about whether they were winners or losers. Just living, being. Sam tried to imagine herself as a fish. She made her mind go blank, and just swam, enjoying the strength of her limbs as they propelled her through the water. Occasionally she'd see some swimmers from the boat. Nobody seemed to need her assistance.

Her father called for all the swimmers to come in and he started the engine again. The next time he stopped the boat it was at a spot with an abundance of stingrays.

"Is it safe?" asked one of the older women, looking over the side of the boat. Below her were two of the strange, black, roundish creatures with their long, whip-like tails. They sat in the water quietly, looking almost sinister.

"As long as you don't try to hang onto their tails or torment them, they're playful as kittens," Mr. O'Neill said.

Paul came up from the cabin with a bucket of chopped conch. "Anyone who is brave can try to feed them," he said. "Hold out the food and they will come to you."

The two teenaged boys were the only ones who took handfuls of conch. Sam scooped up some of the white shellfish and offered it to the older women. "Well, maybe," they said, gingerly picking up pieces of the slippery meat. One of the couples took some conch, too. When the group went over the side of the boat, the stingrays appeared seemingly from nowhere. They were used to Captain Dan's daily visits at this time and were eager to be fed.

Amidst squeals of horror and delight, the people held out the conch and let the velvety stingrays scoop it up. "This is wild," the boy with the longish hair said to Sam when a ray brushed past his legs.

"They're so strange-looking, you wouldn't think they were so gentle," Sam said. Her father had long ago taught her not to be afraid of the rays.

After about forty minutes, they headed for home. Sam resumed her seat at the front of the boat. The boy joined her. "My name is Carl," he said.

"I'm Sam," she introduced herself.

"You're lucky to have such a cool father," he said.

Sam smiled. "You don't think he's a little odd?"

"I think he's great. He seems so relaxed, like he really enjoys his life and his work."

"I think he does," Sam agreed. She looked at her father, laughing with one of the couples as he steered the boat. Was he a winner or a loser?

112

Trisha's father would probably say he was a loser. He didn't earn a lot of money — and he didn't even seem to care. He did seem happy, though.

*Who cares about Trisha, her father, and their stupid system,* Sam thought angrily. *There are other ways of winning besides beating other people.* The boat docked and Paul collected the snorkeling equipment. "I don't think I've ever had this much fun," said one of the older ladies. The rest of the group echoed her sentiment.

"Thank you, thank you all and come again!" said Mr. O'Neill in his best Captain Dan voice.

"Do you work every weekend?" Carl asked Sam.

"I'm not sure," Sam answered. "I was just filling in for someone today."

"Can I call you sometime?" he asked.

Sam tried not to blush. "The number is on the van," she said.

"Okay," the boy said, walking backwards toward the car where his father and brother were waiting. "Nice meeting you."

When the boat was secured and the equipment put away, Sam climbed back into the van with her father. They drove home together, not talking, just listening to the radio. When they pulled into the driveway, Sam noticed a girl standing on her porch.

It was Trisha.

# Chapter Sixteen

"Mind if I don't help you unload the van?" Sam asked her father.

"No, go ahead, talk to your friend," he said.

Sam met Trisha on the porch. "I have to explain to you about today," Trisha said immediately.

"What's there to discuss?" asked Sam. "You double-crossed me. I don't understand why, though."

"That's what I came to tell you," said Trisha. She walked over to the white wicker loveseat on the porch and sat. "You see, I simply couldn't afford to lose that job. I got scared that Mr. Parker would fire me, too, if I seemed to be sticking up for you."

"But you know I didn't push Ismail."

"I know, but I got nervous. If I lose this job, well, Daddy wouldn't understand. He doesn't think much of people who lose." Trisha twirled a piece of her hair around her finger. "Even the thought of having to go home and say I lost the job . . . I couldn't face it, that's all."

"I'm sure your father would — " Sam began.

"No, he wouldn't," Trisha cut her off. "He doesn't tolerate losers."

"Maybe he should," Sam said softly.

"What do you mean?" Trisha asked.

"I mean this loser-winner thing isn't as clear-cut as you make it sound," Sam said passionately. "There are things like being kind, and being happy, and doing things just for the fun of it. Those things count, too."

"I don't know," said Trisha.

"They have to count," said Sam. "I just have to believe that they do."

"Oh, don't get all self-righteous with me!" Trisha snapped. "You don't know what it is to live my life. You can't imagine the pressure of being a Royce. I'm going to inherit a lot of money some day; Daddy is right to insist that I play hard to win. He doesn't want to see me lose my fortune. He doesn't want me to end up like my — " Trisha cut herself short, but Sam could hear the unspoken word, "mother," anyway. Trisha got a hold of herself. "I hope we can still be friends," she said stiffly.

"I lost a job," Sam reminded her. "How can you be friends with a loser?"

"I'm the one who can't be a loser. It's all right for you," Trisha said,

"Thanks a lot," Sam said sarcastically.

"It doesn't matter for people like you," Trisha tried to explain.

"I think I'd like to go inside now," said Sam, not wanting to become totally furious with Trisha. The girl walked off the porch and down the drive. As Sam watched her go, she saw a black Cadillac pull up on the street. Trisha got into it. Sam figured one of Mr. Royce's servants was driving. He must have been circling the block, waiting for Trisha.

She turned into the house, still thinking about Trisha. She had been furious, but suddenly she felt sorry for the girl. She thought about how her own parents had tried to make her feel better when she came home. They hadn't made her feel unloved, or like a failure. Apparently that was what Trisha could expect if she didn't do everything to perfection. That was pretty sad, Sam thought. Sam tried to put herself in Trisha's shoes. Who knew what she would have done in her place? If losing a job had meant feeling unloved by her parents, maybe she would have behaved like a coward, too.

Sam wandered into the kitchen. She looked out the window and saw her mother putting hamburgers on the barbecue in the backyard. Sitting at the kitchen table, she remembered how Chris had told the truth when Mr. Parker was angry at Sam for taking the kids on the beach. She had taken that act of friendship for granted at the time. She realized suddenly that Trisha wasn't the only one with apologies to make. She had been so caught up in her admiration for Trisha that she'd been unfair to Liza and Chris.

She picked up the phone and began to dial. Then she realized there was no dial tone. "What's the matter with this phone?" she asked her mother, who was coming in the back door.

"Trevor pulled out the cord when he was running around with the bag on his head," she told Sam, tearing open another package of chopped meat. "Lloyd is in the back hall trying to fix it now."

"Lloyd is fixing the phone?" Sam asked skeptically.

Not trusting Lloyd's abilities, Sam went outside and got on her bike. She rode for about five minutes until she reached the first public phone booth at a gas station just outside the center of town. She dialed Liza's number. The line was busy. She tried Chris next. That line was also busy. She walked back and forth, watching the cars go by, then she tried again. Both lines were still busy.

They were probably talking to each other, she thought. Or maybe Chris was talking to Bruce and Liza was on the phone with Eddie. She realized she wanted to tell them about that cute boy on the boat, but maybe they wouldn't care. Maybe it was too late and they didn't consider her a friend at all anymore.

After two more tries, Sam gave up and headed for home. She ate on the picnic table out back with her family. She listened halfheartedly as Lloyd tried to explain what he thought was wrong with the phone. She was glad to have such a warm, loving family, but she wanted her friends, too.

The next morning Sam woke up feeling empty. She had already gotten into the habit of getting up early and preparing to go to work. Liza, Chris and Sam had all been scheduled to work on Sundays until one o'clock. She hadn't realized how much she looked forward to seeing Liza and Chris at her door each morning, straddling their bikes, waiting for her to come out.

She got out of bed sleepily and walked to the front door. She looked out. No one was waiting for her and she had no place to go. She stretched and headed for the kitchen.

A sharp rap on the frame of the screen door startled her. She turned around, and there was Liza with her nose pressed up against the screen. "What is wrong with your phone?" she asked irritably.

"Yeah, both of us were trying to call you all last night!" added Chris, coming up behind her.

"It's broken," Sam said. She opened the screen and saw that they were dressed for work.

"Well, hurry up," said Liza. "Parker rehired you. We're going to be late."

Sam's face lit up. "He did! Why?"

Liza and Chris came in and settled on Sam's couch. "We knew you wouldn't push Ismail, so we

118